SMALL TOWN
SECRETS
Allie Harrison

Dear Reader,

Welcome to Mossy Point, where secrets surround the town as well as the dark, abandoned Marston's Tunnel, which seems to be haunted by more than just an unsolved murder. I hope you enjoy your visit, get to know Mac, and say hello to Lizzy when you stop at in the *Bakery & Brew* for a cup of the best coffee and tastiest pie you'll ever have. If you want to know more about me and my books, please check out my Allie Harrison, Author page on Facebook or my website at AllieHarrison.com

Happy Reading,

Allie

Small Town Secrets/Allie Harrison. – 2nd ed.

ISBN 978-1-7375784-5-1

Dedication

To the staff and physicians of the
Belleville Surgery Center. It has been an honor
to work beside you giving excellent patient care.
I will miss you.

Prologue

Eleven years ago, near Marston's Tunnel

Soft light from the truck's dashboard cast an eerie glow over Lizzy Signorino's purple sequin-covered dress, adding radiance to her olive-tanned skin. A song spilled from the radio, telling of being barely seventeen and barely dressed fit the bill.

Not really, James McLane thought. Known as Mac to all his friends, he was more than barely seventeen. He'd be eighteen at Christmas. And, both he and Lizzy were still dressed. Even though he'd brought her to Mossy Point's version of Inspiration Point with high hopes they wouldn't be for much longer. After more than a half hour of kissing beneath little more than the glow of the radio lights on the dashboard, he'd hardly made it to first base.

At least she liked to kiss. And she did it well, despite the metal on her teeth. Her kiss could be enough. He just wished for more. Was there any harm in that?

Mac didn't think so.

He'd finally coaxed her to straddle his lap. She felt good on him. If he could just wish his slacks and belt away...

Her lips were soft and perfect. She tasted of chocolate and mint. Nice. Good. Making him hunger for more. She had a leg on each side of his; he rested a hand on each of her perfect calves. Smooth, soft muscle, firm. He wanted to touch her everywhere. With eyes closed, his mouth moving on hers, he slid his hands up her legs from ankles to knees. Just a few inches more and he could slip up and touch her thighs.

Then he would be all that much closer to her heat he felt through the material of his slacks. He still couldn't believe he was here with her. This close, almost to the point he could put his hands up the skirt of her beautiful dress.

He almost felt dirty parking with her out near the old train tunnel, known as Marston's Tunnel. It was where all the local teenagers parked. It was where he'd taken Kelly Mattis.

But damn, he wanted to be alone with Lizzy. He wanted her all to himself. At the dance, he'd seen all the other guys—his teammates—ogling over her. He'd also noticed how most of the girls, including Kelly Mattis, his date from last year's prom, looked ready to kill him, too. Wanting to avoid the bitch, who'd chosen to wear a slinky, hot pink number, he'd held Lizzy closer as they danced slow.

The effort wasn't fast enough. He had seen the hate in Kelly's eyes.

Now, he concentrated on the girl on his lap.

She wasn't like any other girl he'd been with.

Mac managed to slide his right hand up her thigh. So many sensations at once...

The pressure and heat and sweetness of her kiss.

The silkiness of the dress material on the back of his hand.

Soft, warm skin beneath his palm.

Lace against his fingertips.

He wondered what color her panties were. Purple to match the dress? Flesh tone to blend in? White, which would in no way be boring on her? Pink, because he was pretty certain every girl owned a pair of pink panties?

His heart raced in his chest, and he moaned into her kiss. He was pretty sure he was touching a little piece of heaven.

The song on the radio ended. Had the guy in the song gotten lucky and slid into home plate? He couldn't remember. What he did remember was a saying his dad had told him once. "Enjoy the journey as much as the destination."

He certainly was.

The new song was something slower.

Seeming to keep pace with it, he ended his kiss and leaned back. Her face was shadowed.

His right hand refusing to leave the heat of her thigh, he cupped her face with his left. Wow, she was soft everywhere he touched. "You're beautiful," he whispered.

He couldn't see it in the shadows, but he'd bet his paycheck he earned baling hay that she blushed. He felt the heat where he touched her cheek. The late-night fall breeze smelled of dry leaves and blew the trees surrounding the tunnel. Speckles of moonlight danced about the truck like a kaleidoscope. Lizzy smiled. He wished time could stop right here, right now, so he could stay with her like this. It was an odd feeling, not *needing* to find out what secrets she held under her panties. In a very short matter of time, she had become too important to him for that. There was more to her, so many layers he wanted to explore.

"In case I forget to tell you, I had a really nice time tonight," she said softly.

"Me, too."

He leaned forward to kiss her again, but she tensed suddenly and her gasp made him forget about the kiss. "What?"

"I saw a light coming from the Tunnel."

She peered over his shoulder. He felt her breasts flattened closer against him, as she leaned closer, trying to see. It was so nice, but her next words doused the fire in him. "There was a light. And I saw someone. I think it was a man."

The fear in her voice sent a chill through him. No one he knew ventured into Marston's Tunnel. Not anymore. The place was creepy. Years ago, probably sometime before he was born, the train tracks had been removed up as far as the entrance of the tunnel. The brick mouth of the tunnel was old and moist. Moss and unidentifiable vegetation grew out from between the bricks, adding to the creepy feeling. The talk he'd heard all his life living in Mossy Point was that the place was haunted, that when trains entered one end, they never come out the other.

And that people did the same.

The fact that Lizzy saw someone step out, or a light, sent a chill through him.

He shifted, staring toward the tunnel, trying to see through the darkness. There was nothing but dancing shadows and pitch black where he knew the opening of the tunnel sat waiting. He stared hard, waiting, almost willing there to be something more.

Then he saw it, too.

Just a flash. And he recognized it.

Someone switched on a flashlight. Just for half a heartbeat. On...Off.

Whomever it was allowed a bit of light to pave the way. And did Mac see the dark figure of a person in the brief peek of light? He thought so.

Regretfully, he gently slid Lizzy off his lap and onto the bench seat beside him. He fought down another shiver, but he didn't know if it was from the sudden cool that hit him with the loss of her heat, or the fact someone besides them was there. Hell, with the way their focus had been on each other for the last half hour, whomever it was could have been watching them through the window of his truck, and they wouldn't have noticed.

That didn't answer the question. Who was in Marston's Tunnel? And why?

He grasped the door handle, but her hand on his leg stopped him like a sprinter skidding in soft gravel. She leaned over him and locked the door. "No, don't open the door. We don't know why anyone's even out here. Why would anyone go into the tunnel in the middle of the night?"

He should have had the doors locked anyway. His dad was the Chief of Police. He knew better than anyone no one was safe anywhere.

"You're right." He thought for a long moment. He locked the other door, too, although it was clear no one was out that direction.

Whomever it was, was in the tunnel. "I need to call my dad and let him know someone was in the tunnel."

"No. Take me home first."

"I can't do that. Whomever it is will be long gone. And my dad would want to know someone was in there in the middle of the night."

"Your dad will know we were here," she argued. "Besides, maybe it's nothing. Maybe it's just someone walking home and taking a short cut."

"No one takes a short cut through Marston's Tunnel. Who would be walking home this time of night? And where would they be coming from?" He took her hand. "It'll be okay. I gotta tell him. If something happened and I didn't tell him—it would be worse. He'll believe me when I tell him we didn't do anything more than kiss. It'll be okay."

He used speed dial to reach his dad. Both of them watched the tunnel for more light, any other activity. He saw none.

His dad answered his cell with "You okay, son?"

"We're okay, but..."

"Did your truck break down?"

Mac knew the sound of worry in his dad's voice. "No, but..."

Hell, he might as well get it over with. "First of all, I want to tell you that nothing happened. I mean nothing with Lizzy. She and I are up at Marston's Tunnel. All we did was kiss. I promise." *That wasn't so bad*, he thought and let out the breath he'd been holding. "But we just saw a light and a guy down in the tunnel."

"Both you and Lizzy are okay?"

"Yeah."

"Are your doors locked?"

"Yeah."

"Are you facing a direction you can leave in a hurry?"

"Yeah."

"Start your truck, keep your eyes open. If you see anything else, you get the hell out of there. I'm on that side of town and on my way. ETA three minutes."

It amazed him how authoritative his dad could sound.

Mac started the truck. "Got the truck started."

"Good."

"Are we leaving?" Lizzy asked.

"Not yet. My dad will want to know where we were and where we saw the light. We'll leave if we see anything or anyone else."

It was a long three minutes. Mac let out another long-held breath when the headlights of his dad's police car shined through the trees of the winding road that led to where he and Lizzy were. The siren was off, but the lights on top sent blue spots reflecting off the fall leaves of the trees. He heard Lizzy's intake of breath when a second set of headlights and more flashing lights followed, but Mac knew how his dad worked. He wouldn't come alone. He'd always have backup, even if it was something that could be a false alarm. It was probably Tyson. Mac was pretty certain Tyson was on duty on Saturday nights.

His dad parked so his headlights shined into the mouth of the dragon.

Mac opened the door and climbed out, standing beside his truck, leaving the door open in case he needed to jump back in in a hurry. Lizzy slid out beside him.

Tyson, or whoever it was, drove alongside Mac's dad and parked so double the light flooded the tunnel.

Again, he heard Lizzy's gasp. Her face was still hidden in the shadows, but the light reflected in her green eyes. Mac followed her gaze into the Marston's Tunnel. For the first time, with the tunnel lit up, he saw the bricks that created the mouth of the tunnel were dark gray with age. The tunnel wasn't long, perhaps the length of an average city block. Four bright beams were enough to funnel light to the other side.

The light touched on something.

Something hot and neon pink.

Mac's gut twisted. Kelly Mattis had worn a dress that color to the dance. He hadn't seen anyone else with a dress that same color. Of course not. Girls talked. Everyone would know what the 'popular' girls planned to wear to the dance, and no one would dare to wear the same color.

Dear God...was that a splotch of red covering the bright pink material?

Lizzy was suddenly in his arms. He didn't want to look. He wanted to just hold Lizzy. Couldn't they just go back to ten minutes ago?

No.

It was a life-altering moment for James McLane. One that would haunt him and be the object of his nightmares for many nights to come.

Chapter One

Almost eleven years later.

Monday

Mac stepped off his parents' back porch and paused to take in the beauty of the orchard. The leaves of flourishing trees rustled in the breeze. Tractor tire ruts marked a path for him to follow, and the sweet aroma of apples in the warm fall morning sunshine made him feel like a little boy again. He took in a deep breath and smiled. This is the smell of home.

He saw his dad, Former Chief of Police Robert McLane, a short distance away out strolling amongst rows of trees, checking the apples in the orchard he'd planted when Mac had been a little boy. Robert had always wanted an orchard; it seemed like the perfect thing for him after retirement.

"Good morning, son. Did you sleep well?"

"The loft apartment you put above the barn is perfect."

Ozzie, his parents' golden retriever, cantered over to greet Mac, who spent a few seconds giving the faithful dog a good scratch under his chin and on his belly.

As he petted the dog, he realized his dad seldom called him by his first name. Even that night when he'd had to call and say he and Lizzy were at Marston's Tunnel—and he was certain his dad damn sure knew what he had in mind when he took Lizzy there—his dad had just said, "Both you and Lizzy are okay, son?"

The next morning, after what had obviously been a night of filling out reports and calling in the Major Crime Squad, his dad had given him something close to a hug.

Now, Mac greeted him with the same. "I don't know if I've ever told you, but I love everything about this orchard. The air smells cleaner. I can feel the trees soaking up the sunshine."

His dad grinned. "Yes, it's my favorite place, too. And it's doing well. We had a great crop of peaches this summer. You should have seen the giant strawberries, too."

"What are you doing now?"

"Checking the apples. We have a bumper crop of those, too, this year. Which is good, since I have bales of straw set up in a maze. In the next few weeks, we'll be inundated with school kids here on field trips to pick apples. After that, it'll be pumpkins. I don't get many to grow well, so I always have a few truckloads delivered."

Keeping pace with Robert, Mac admired his dad's hard work in the way of what were rows of spotless, perfect apples. Ozzie's tail thumped against Mac's leg as the dog loped beside him for a moment before he sauntered off to sniff something under a nearby tree. Mac watched his dad. Retirement was obviously a great thing for his dad. Against the white tee shirt he wore, Robert was tanned and healthy from working outdoors. The only thing that revealed his age was his dark hair giving way to something close to salt and pepper. To Mac, he sounded so much more at ease than he had as Chief.

"How's the leg?" his dad asked.

"Getting better every day, especially if I walk enough steps so it doesn't get the chance to stiffen up."

"Good." Robert picked an apple, rubbed it against his shirt, and took a bite. "Your mother didn't get much sleep when we heard."

"I know. I'm sorry. I never meant to worry either of you."

"It's nice you came home for a while so we could see for ourselves." They were quiet for several steps before Robert said, "I can see you've got something deeper than apples and our worry on your mind. What is it?"

It was one trait that made his dad a great cop, Mac thought. His ability to read people. "The Kelly Mattis case."

"Ugh." His father grasped a nearby apple on a branch without picking it. After he gave it a thorough inspection, he released it and took a bite of the one he held in his other hand, and trekked on.

Then Robert chuckled bitterly. "You'd think after ten years, her murder wouldn't bother me. Even after staying out here soaking up the sunshine..." He sighed. Loudly. And let his thought die as he closed his eyes and tipped his head up, as if the sunlight shining down could take way the dark of Kelly's murder.

Mac listened to chirping birds and bit his lip. He hated more than anything to bring this back up to his dad. It was a dark time, and he felt like he opened an old wound.

Then Robert took a deep breath and again met Mac's gaze. "So, what do you want to know and why? I thought you were coming here for a rest while your leg heals and to just attend your reunion." Then he gave Mac a hard, studied stare. "You're working the case, aren't you?"

Mac shrugged, feeling like he'd been caught with his hand in the cookie jar. "Kind of. I thought since I was back, I could check out a few things, see if I could gain any insight. Besides, it gives me something to think about besides my damned leg aching." *Or Lizzy.* "Like everything else I've told you in the last decade, you have to keep it to yourself."

Robert grinned. "Oh, yes. That undercover, classified stuff. Your mom and I don't even tell our friends when we take a vacation and visit you for fear we might get too many questions. We haven't even told anyone you were shot. Is there some reason you needed to keep everything hidden? Why couldn't you have just gone through the academy and become Chief when I retired?"

It was Mac's turn to grin. He added a shrug. "I don't know, Dad. It's just the way it worked out. You know how it is. You take one certain test in college and score a certain score and, the next thing you know, the FBI is knocking. Then they notice you're really good with falling into rolls and playing undercover. So suddenly that's what your job is."

His dad chuckled. "It didn't quite work that way, did it?"

"Not quite," Mac replied. "But close."

"If you ever decide to give up keeping secrets, you can always come home for good. And I bet you could even take up residence in my old office at some point. Hell, you can even just set up straw bales for the little kids who want to pick apples."

"Maybe I might. Especially if I can never run very far very fast again."

He gazed around at the orchard and breathed in a deep breath of fresh apple air. And the idea of staying here and enjoying this while no one shot at him suddenly sounded damned appealing to him. A flash of a little house with a picket fence on the other side of the orchard slithered through his mind. A home, with a wife and family. With Lizzy. He could even help her in her bakery.

Mac halted that thought like a small fire doused with a bucket of water. Why Lizzy Signorino invaded his thoughts since a bullet entered his body, he couldn't fathom. More than once, he couldn't help but wonder just where he would have ended up if it hadn't been for Kelly Mattis's murder, or if he and Lizzy hadn't been outside the tunnel that night. At the same time, he questioned why thoughts of Lizzy came to the surface when he thought he might be dying. He told himself he was thinking these thoughts because he was actually tired of keeping all the secrets. He was tired of being undercover. He was tired with the fact that his life and his job seemed like little more than a lie all the time. It wasn't because of Lizzy or because he'd never gotten any closure with her. No, it was because Kelly Mattis's murder had somehow torn a hole through the middle of his life. And he needed to claw his way beyond it. Lizzy was just another jagged edge of that tear, one that he planned to easily smooth out and leave behind. The sooner, the better.

He swallowed hard, knowing he could do that, just as he'd done every other job he'd worked in the past decade. The catch in his leg caused him to step lightly.

The sun was getting warmer as it rose in the sky. Ozzie sauntered up and stuck a cold nose to his leg—not the sore one. Mac felt it through his jeans before he leaned down to give his ears scratch. The dog seemed to be saying, *I feel your pain. I'm here for you.*

"I could probably get my reports and the entire file on Kelly Mattis from Chief Daniels," Robert suggested. "I could tell him I just wanted to compare a note or two so no one would know you were trying to heat up a cold case."

"I already have the entire file, every official report. And I don't want to say anything to Chief Daniels or anyone else. No one can know what I'm doing here, even the cops in town. Hell, Jake Swornson, is now on the police force. We played sports together back in high school. I'm pretty sure he was one of Kelly's 'dates.' What I need are your notes, whatever extra you had."

When his dad said nothing, Mac continued. "I know how you worked. I know how you still work. Little notes here and there, just thoughts, random." He let out a light chuckle. "You kept an entire notebook of random thoughts. Just like I do. And you still have a notebook sitting on your desk at home. I'm sure you have an entire notebook on the Kelly Mattis case alone—maybe even two of them. I doubt you handed them over to anyone. I wouldn't be surprised if you didn't sit and read them every night."

Bored with their conversation, Ozzie lay down not far from Mac's feet, rolled over and rubbed his back in the grass.

His dad gave him a hard glance before shifting his gaze to the orchard.

Mac pretended to watch Ozzie.

Then his father did a good job of pretending to check the apples on the nearest tree for a long moment. Ozzie jumped to his feet and followed. Robert gave the dog a pet. "I used to read the two notebooks. That case tore at me, like nothing else I've ever faced. Things like that didn't happen in little mid-western towns like ours. Not on my watch.

I questioned everyone—even you and that pretty girl you had parked not far from that tunnel. When I think about you being that close to a killer, my heart feels like it might pop like a balloon in my chest."

"I think everyone in town has been that close to the killer."

Robert shifted his attention to Mac, his expression narrowing. "Do you know something new? Did you pick up on a clue that I missed in all the reports?"

"Kind of. Maybe. I think it might be connected to another murder."

"*Another* murder?"

He hated like hell to tell Robert. Worse, he hated the way the color disappeared from his dad's face. Robert blanched as if Mac just punched him in the gut.

"Are you sure they're connected?" The question was nothing more than a whisper.

Mac shrugged. "Not positive. Only by time and place...and my gut."

"That would make our killer a serial killer. My God."

"I know."

"How?" Robert asked.

"Between every other case I've worked, I was always reading your report, just like you, and searching for something that maybe was missed, something that needed further investigation. Kelly was at the dance. She didn't have a date. And no one remembered seeing her leave. Lizzy and I both only saw one person inside the tunnel that night, apparently that person saw my truck parked there, and back tracked the other way and escaped, leaving no clue, just a stabbed girl. And Dad, there's the question of her finances."

Robert's brows knit together in question. "What about her finances?"

"I found a report done by the Major Case Squad stating she had several thousand dollars in a savings account. It was a lot, I thought, for a teenage girl who never had a paying job. At least a job where she filed income taxes. For a girl who was the daughter of a single mother who struggled to make ends meet, I haven't been able to find a single thing that tells me where she got the money."

"I don't recall that report."

"Dad, I've thought and thought about it. Her killer had to be someone she trusted. No one I know ventured into that creepy tunnel. Kelly would have never gone into that place. Not without good reason."

"I've gone over it again and again, and I can't think of a reason for her to be there. No one even knew when she left the dance. What was the clue that tipped you off and made you try and connect it to other crimes, to another murder?"

"It wasn't really a single clue. I started putting information into a database, just making something of a map, putting in every remote piece of information to see if any of the dots connected. I put in what I knew—where townspeople, the people in my graduating class, were during specific spans of time to see if there were any other unsolved murders."

"Why do you think it was someone in your class?"

"This."

From his back pocket Mac took out a folded, printed photo, unfolded it, and handed it to his father. Kelly Mattis's lifeless eyes stared up at the camera. Her bloody torso was covered with open gashes. Her pink dress was red. Her left arm was stretched above her head, her right lay across her waist. The bricks of the tunnel surrounding her body were splattered with her blood.

Robert glanced down. "Ah, the picture that plagues my nightmares. What about it?"

"A few months ago after I finished a case, I studied the photos. Normally, I just read reports. When I examined this one closer, I remembered something she said long ago. Why I remembered it then, I have no idea. I guess I was so busy seeing all her blood and the horror of it, I didn't notice anything else or any of the details on her. But...shortly before the end of my junior year, I took her to Marston Tunnel."

When Robert gave him another sharp look, Mac held up his hands in a defensive motion. "I know. I know. You taught me better than that. I have no excuse. I was a hormone-raging teenage boy and she was a girl willing and eager to put out. I knew she gave it away to all the guys. And if it's any consolation, it didn't really have the happy ending like you think. What's important was she told me if she could, she'd make me give her my class ring, which I wouldn't have done anyway. When I asked her why she didn't *make* me, she told me she was very allergic to metal against her skin, almost any metal."

Robert glanced down at the photo again. "She's wearing a bracelet."

"Yes, a bracelet I didn't notice because I was too busy noticing everything else. Her parents never saw because it was put into an evidence box. Otherwise, I'm sure her mom would have picked up on it."

"Shit." Robert let out a long breath. "What's engraved on it?"

"Number One, using the pound symbol and the numeral."

"That's it?"

Mac shook his head slightly. "Yep."

"And you think the killer's someone in town? Why?"

Mac took the photo from his father and pointed down at the bracelet. "Aside from the little engraved part with the number one, see this upside-down heart?"

Robert studied it closer. "Yes."

"That was a mistake on the part of the manufacturer. I remember seeing all the supplies to make jewelry in metal working class. Mr. Crinden, our teacher even explained that he got most of those supplies at a discount because there were flaws in them, one being that the hearts were upside down. Now I'm sure other metal working class teachers bought them in other schools to save money, too. And maybe I'm taking a leap in the wrong direction, but it's a big coincidence that a dead girl who was allergic to metal would be wearing a bracelet made from pieces I remember from a high school class. I don't believe in coincidence."

"You saw these bracelets?" Robert asked. "These jewelry pieces?"

Mac hesitated for a moment, and then could find no better words. "I made one."

"Sweet Heavens."

That hadn't been what Mac had said when he'd focused on the bracelet and remembered. As if Ozzie had been left out of the conversation too long, he cantered over Mac's right foot. When Mac ignored him, he pranced to Robert.

His dad stooped down and rubbed Ozzie with gusto as if he needed to touch something warm and soft and loving after receiving such news. He shook his head in disbelief. "Then we need to check out everyone who took metal working class and made jewelry."

"I already did that."

His dad still petted the dog. "And?"

"It added names to my list of suspects. I couldn't remember who was with whom at the dance. And that doesn't even count anyone who could have gotten their hands on the jewelry."

Mac watched his dad. Ozzie, who was oblivious to the horror of their conversation, pretty much enfolded his body against Robert's leg, gaining all the attention he could. "That's why I need your notes. I need to know who you thought might be holding something back or who might be lying so I can compare them to my long list. And I also need to compare notes so I can see if anything connects to where she got all the money in her account."

"You must have someone in mind since I could have simply sent you my notebook," his father pointed out.

"I needed to come back anyway. I needed to let myself heal, and something told me this was the best place to do it. A lot of things flashed through my mind when I was lying there on a gurney thinking

I might not make it." Like all the things he'd left unsaid to people he knew.

"I'll bet."

"On top of that, one of my classmates attended to the University of Missouri, and the second unsolved murder victim I found lived in Columbia, Missouri, and had also taken a few classes at the University of Missouri. This classmate also took wood shop class and metal shop class."

"Who's that?"

"Lizzy's brother."

It amazed him how after he'd been shot, Lizzy climbed to the top of his thoughts. He didn't think Tony Signorino. He thought *Lizzy's brother*.

"Hell and damnation," his dad let out like a sad, frustrated sigh.

"Ain't that the truth?" *Hell*. It was certainly where he felt this case, and the two bullets that left their scars on him, and the hole left by Lizzy, had placed him.

When Robert attempted to stand, Ozzie put a paw on him, as if the action would keep the rub down coming. The dog wagged his tail and panted up happily.

Oh, to have the life of a dog, Mac thought.

Chapter Two

On his drive into town, Mac remembered every detail about homecoming night as if it happened yesterday.

It was one of the nicest nights of his life, and it had started out as a dare. His best friend, Kyle, had dared him to even speak to Lizzy Signorino. Of course, everyone knew her. Her father, after all, owned and operated the only bakery in town. He didn't think the little mousy Lizzy Signorino could speak, much less utter an intelligent word. He was certain that in three years of high school, he'd never seen her without her nose buried in a book. She always seemed to work to be invisible. And, as far as everyone seemed concerned, she was. So, when he told Kyle he needed a 'worthy' girl to take to the homecoming dance, Kyle jokingly said, "You should ask the little Italian baker. Her dad might give you some free donuts or something. After all, you should give the loser girls a chance, too, now and then."

He'd looked across the hall to where the *little Italian baker* stood at her locker. She wasn't like other girls. She didn't have a mirror stuck on the inside of her locker door. Her hair, which was the color of gold honey with hints of red spun in, was held back in a simple pony tail. She grabbed her physics book and hurried away, not noticing he watched her. And sarcastically he thought *I should give her a chance. It's senior year. She'll probably never get another chance to attend a dance, at least with the assistant captain of the football team.* As assistant captain of the football team, he should be generous.

"Why not?" he'd muttered.

He remembered it had taken him several steps as he followed her for him to recall her name and not actually call her *little Italian baker*. His request to accompany him to the homecoming dance must have floored her. She'd stared at him for a whole ten seconds, making him think she really couldn't speak.

Then she'd replied, very politely, in a voice he thought was only given to angels, "I would love to go with you, thank you."

There'd been something in her eyes. Something almost physical that grabbed him and held tight. And this was no longer a dare, nothing close to a prank. He'd found himself drawn to her. He'd grinned, feeling glad he'd acted. He'd found himself quietly looking forward to the dance.

Then he'd been the one who was floored and speechless when he'd come to her door to pick her up, a purple and white flower wrist corsage in his hands. Her hair was pinned up, decorated with tiny pearls, wisps framing her face. Her eyes were brilliantly green and large on her face, her skin flawless.

She'd obviously been hiding all that beauty, although he had no idea where.

A few simple thoughts had flashed through his mind as he stood there dumbfounded staring at her.

She's with me.

She's going to dance with me. And no one else is going to get close to her.

She's mine.

Then her father, the baker, who stood holding the door open to him, spoke and broke the spell she'd cast on him. "I trust you will keep my daughter safe, Mr. McLane."

He'd had to blink and clear his throat before he could croak out, "Yes, sir."

Her mother had insisted on pictures.

Mac barely remembered them being taken. He was pretty sure they'd floated through the dance, and he couldn't recall what he'd eaten when he took her to dinner.

It had been eleven long years. He thought it was all behind him. Then two shots had been fired, two shots that left him bleeding, possibly dying, and certainly questioning his life's work, and so many things about his life—his high school years, his stupid decisions, his one wonderful/horrible night with Lizzy popped back into thoughts as if they happened yesterday. Now, as he drove through his hometown, he remembered every detail.

From the soft, flowery scent of Lizzy's hair and the lacy touch of her panties under her dress to the nightmare of knowing someone had used a knife on Kelly Mattis, to the harsh but deadly quiet sound of Lizzy's father accusing him of breaking his word and putting Lizzy in danger.

"You are never to see my daughter again. You are never to date her. You are never to speak to her. Do you understand?"

There had been an unspoken message in Mr. Signorino's eyes and a sound in his heavy Italian accent that said Mac would regret it if he didn't understand. Chief's son or not, there had been no doubt he'd better listen to this father.

He also remembered the way Lizzy had gazed at him as her father held her by one arm and dragged her out of the police station when he'd come to get her. It hadn't mattered that both he and Lizzy had pleaded that nothing happened between them, only kissing.

I'm sorry, her expression said.

He'd wanted more than anything to talk to her throughout the year, but he held back, her father's voice ringing in his head like a bell. He couldn't help but notice she had no classes with him. She avoided him.

He didn't venture into the bakery again. Ever. He knew, through others, her father had her working every minute that wasn't needed to finish homework.

Damn, if he had known how much crap either of them would have to endure for doing nothing, he'd have sure well done *something* more than enjoy her kiss. He'd spent many nights the rest of that senior year wondering if she felt the same.

Then he'd poured himself into college and his job.

His hometown and the life he'd left here only crashed back as he lay bleeding.

It amazed him how his town could be different but the same. The Mossy Point Pharmacy was exactly the same. The Quick Step Gas Stop was now The Quicker Liquor store. Mac guessed they discovered they made more money on booze than on gas. He chuckled over the name. The library was bigger, and he remembered his mother telling him how she helped get the new children's library addition. The Streetside Bar was one of those smoky, dusty places that he was certain never changed. He passed the high school. And he swore he thought he could smell the wood floor of the gymnasium.

As he slowed for the in-town limit, he rolled his window down and was taken aback. The town *smelled* the same, fresh and kind of earthy, like woods, like home mixed with a crisp scent of burning leaves. He passed the house where he'd lived when he was little before the purchase of the orchard. It was now owned by a young couple with little kids as his mother had told him. There was a For Sale sign in front of it. He wondered if the wall where his mother had marked his and his brother's growth charts had been painted over. Probably.

He drove into the crowded parking lot of Lizzy's father's bakery, stopped, and killed the engine. Yes, he planned to say unsaid words to Lizzy. He wasn't even certain what those words were, but he knew she was an open file that he needed to close. He hadn't really planned to start here at her bakery, but he knew of no other place better.

The bakery was familiar and new at the same time, given the new sign. He knew without a doubt that Lizzy was behind the new sign, and probably behind any and all changes. *Signorino's Bakery and Brew.* The building still held its quaint appeal, but there was new paint and a welcoming display of wooden chairs and teacups on a small table in the window.

There was a fancy chalkboard sign beside the door. *Today's Special Vanilla Latte and Apple Pie. Come in and choose a book to borrow from our library.*

Yes, Lizzy would be behind the changes in the place. He could almost touch the memory of her holding a book and reading as she advanced to her next class through the hall of high school, trying to get a few words in as she made her way to her next class.

He didn't know about a vanilla latte. To him, coffee was coffee. He liked it strong and hot and black. Apple pie was his favorite.

His leg ached as he climbed out of his truck. Would it ever heal? Would it ever be the same? He would never have guessed such a small thing as a bullet could cause so much pain.

Or make him question his career choices.

Or give him nightmares.

Or be enough to send him back to his hometown. At least he didn't feel like a dog with his tail tucked between his legs.

He sucked in a deep breath and worked to ignore the burn in his thigh. It was strange, he thought as he headed to the door, that the second bullet, the one that entered his left mid-section and required longer surgery, and longer healing given the vital organs in that vicinity, didn't hurt at all anymore.

Bells over the door tinkled lightly and musically to announce his arrival. Everyone in the place paused in sipping their coffee and stared at him. Back in his football days, he would've loved and lived for the attention. He'd probably have waved like a king in a parade.

He was no longer that football jock who thought he had the world by a string. Now, ambling in, everyone studying him as he did his best not to let his limp show its ugly head, he felt like some sort of a traitor. The guy who'd escaped the town, escaped the dark cloud that hung over it. And he didn't want anyone seeing him come back in.

He forced a glad-to-be-here-again smile on his lips and gave everyone a wave. Some faces he recognized. Mr. Witherbee, who used to be known as the cafeteria police at the high school. Mac had thought he was ancient a decade ago. He hadn't changed a bit. He sat at a table with Jack Hitchcock, who was still the principal, and who appeared older with white hair and a gauntly hollowness to his face as if the job was taking its toll on him. Mrs. Hamilton, who grew the prettiest roses in a greenhouse for the florist. There was a family he didn't recognize—husband, wife, baby, and little kid too young to be in school. A few other familiar people sat at tables. Four people sat in recliners at the far end of the bakery. Bookshelves and books were beyond them as they sat with books in their hands and steaming cups of drinks on small tables nearby.

He took in the counter, which was new and had six anchored stools in front of it. He didn't recall them being there. The colorful, decorative menu, painted with chalkboard paint complete with prices and flowers and smiley faces and pictures of mugs of steaming brew which filled the entire back wall behind the counter was new, too.

Stan Gresden, one of his best friends from high school, captain for the football team, the only person who was probably a bigger jock than him back in the day wore a gray uniform shirt and sat on one of the stools with a coffee cup poised, ready to drink. "Is that you, Mac? Damn, look what the cat dragged in!"

"Hey, Stan," Mac let out as if he'd only been gone a few days, instead of over a decade. Relaxed—or at least trying to be—he extended his hand. Stan shook it with a great deal of enthusiasm. Stan's brother, Elliot, sat on the stool on Stan's other side. Mac shook his hand, too. "Elliot."

"M-m-maac," Elliot let out. He pumped Mac's hand vigorously. "I-it's g-g-good to see you. I've missed you."

"It's good to see you, too, buddy." Elliot was a year older, but was in a special education class, and Stan had always acted more like the big brother. And Mac remembered how all the guys on the football team accepted Elliot and allowed him to be the water boy, making him part of the team.

"You've hardly aged a day," Stan commented.

"You look pretty good yourself."

"And to think we were supposed to make it to State together. We didn't make it, did we?"

Mac gave a nonchalant shrug. "Sometimes plans fall through." He climbed onto a stool, wondering just how much his damned leg would ache if he'd played more football and gained painful knees on top of the injury he now suffered.

It was the woman behind the counter who grabbed Mac's attention. Perhaps grabbed wasn't the complete sensation. More like grabbed, held, and squeezed until he could barely take a breath.

Lizzy Signorino, wearing a white blouse with the sleeves rolled up, a pair of sweet jeans that hugged her curves and a white apron that failed to hide those curves, stared at him as if she'd seen a ghost. Her braces of high school were gone from her teeth. Her wavy, strawberry blond hair was held up by some kind of clip. Tiny wisps escaped to dangle around both ear lobes. And those glorious emerald eyes. Wide and...wary?

Fighting off the feeling that threatened to overload him, he worked to relax on the stool. "Hi, Lizzy."

"Mac..."

He smiled at her, but his face felt tight, uncomfortable, his jaw as painful as his leg as he still felt caught in whatever net she'd easily tossed over him. At least he could breathe. "Would you mind if I had a cup of coffee from the pot you've got in your hand?"

She blinked as if seeing him had put her in a trance. Then she grabbed a nearby cup and poured the coffee. He noticed her hand was shaking.

He sure as hell hoped he sounded calmer than he felt, and he had the feeling his hand would shake if he tried to pour coffee. He studied the picturesque menu beyond her, but nothing connected. This was not what he planned. The return of any feelings for Lizzy was a surprise. He was over her. There was no reason for her to be shaking. There was no reason for him to think he'd be shaking either.

Get over it, Mac. There has been a lot of water pass under that bridge. Don't even try to go back. That'd be like making a touchdown for the wrong team.

He cleared his throat, telling himself football for him was over, too. "What's good here?"

"It's all good here," Stan said. "Have a piece of Lizzy's apple pie. It's the best." He leaned closer. "It's even better than my mom's, but don't tell her."

"Your secret's safe with me. I'll have a piece of pie."

He noticed Lizzy, although free of her frozen stance, still stared at him. He was certain he could smell her perfume under the heavy scent of pastry. How strange, he thought. The scent of her took him back in an instant as nothing else. He'd spent the last ten years doing his job, falling into rolls and pretending to be something—someone—else, and he'd done it well, putting the bad guys where they belonged.

Now, he stepped into the bakery and managed to go back in time, or perhaps entered a place where time had stopped. For a moment, he concentrated on taking a breath as he tucked aside the feeling he was once again that quarterback on the football team instead of the man he was. Those days were over, and he had no desire to ever return.

Not that he could anyway. That life was miles of water under the bridge. Lizzy, the young girl of his high school days was gone.

But she'd been replaced by something better.

Even if he hadn't known her ten years ago, he'd still be staring at her as he was now.

"So where have you been all this time?" Stan asked.

"Here and there, no place special. My mom mentioned there was a ten-year reunion coinciding with the Mossy Point Days Picnic this coming weekend, so I'd thought I'd check out the old stomping grounds for a week or two."

The lie slid easily from his lips. It would be more than a week or two if he couldn't get his head back in the game. And if he couldn't run a few yards without his leg being on fire.

"Are you staying with them—your mom and dad?"

"They've got an apartment over the barn. It's got a comfortable bed, plumbing, and a hot shower. I thought I'd spend my time there so I don't have to be in their way." Mac didn't add that they had all but begged him to stay in the house, but he knew he was going to need some space. At least he thought he needed space. Right now, sitting in the bakery, trying to ignore memories he thought he was over, he didn't know what he needed.

He'd never left a job undone, and he wasn't starting now. He'd figure out what to say to Lizzy to close that door that had opened as he thought he might die. He'd study the Kelly Mattis case, he'd spend some time with his family and see some old friends at a reunion, and then he'd get out of Dodge.

The reunion was a good excuse and a great change of subject. He took a sip of coffee and nodded to Lizzy. "Good coffee."

She nodded back. Her smile didn't quite meet her eyes. She set the coffee pot back on the coffee maker and took a few steps to the pie case where she removed an apple pie with a couple of slices gone.

On the counter, not far away, she sliced him a piece. "Whipped cream or ice cream?"

"Neither, thank you."

Good God, the formality was so thick in the room, he could have cut it with the knife she held in her hand.

"Do you think while you're here, Mac, we could climb to the top and sit on the water tower for a while like we used to?" Elliot asked, only stuttering a few words. "I don't think we've done that since you left."

Mac paused in taking another sip of coffee, and thought *thank God for Elliot*. "I think we can fit that in, Elliot. We can even get a few other guys to go with us, whoever's in town for the picnic or reunion. Do you think you can make it all the way to the top?" He wasn't certain his leg could handle the ladder, but maybe what he needed was to start forcing it to do what he wanted it to do.

"Sure," Elliot replied.

"I'm in," Stan said.

"Me, too." Lizzy's brother, Tony, approached from somewhere near the back of the bakery. He reached out to shake Mac's hand. "Nice to see you."

The conversation turned relaxed, filled with memories.

"Remember that last game before I hurt my knee," Stan said, "That was the best. We whipped the pants off those Hornets."

"That we did," said Mac.

"You guys drank all my water. I had to go back and refill my jug two times," Elliot added. He only stuttered on the G and J sounds.

"Good thing you were there to have it for us, Elliot," Mac put in, making Elliot beam with pride.

Stan put down his mug with a thud. "We gotta get back to the shop."

"What? You gotta go back and put out some cat food?" Jason Oglesvie called out from a few tables away.

Most of the people in the place chuckled. Elliot laughed, and then answered. "We put out food for all of them, but they still do a great job catching mice. I like that gray tabby cat. I call her Tiger even though she's a girl. She lets me pet her."

Stan folded his napkin, set his coffee cup on it, and placed his spoon inside before he clapped his hand on Elliot's shoulder. Mac remembered Stan used to place his football equipment in his locker in a certain order, too.

"Come on, Elliot. We need to get back to work. Nice to see you again, Mac. I'm sure we'll see more of you during the week. Stop in at the body shop if you want. You know I'm still running it, ever since my dad left town," Stan said

"And I help," Elliot added.

"And Elliot helps," Stan chimed.

"I know." Mac took a sip of his coffee.

"We'll have to share a beer or two up at the Streetside Bar before you head out again."

"Streetside's still up and running?" Mac asked, even though he'd seen it driving in.

"Stronger than ever," Stan said.

Elliot giggled. "We used to get beer there before we were legal," he said as if it was a big secret, and he only stuttered on the L in legal.

"That we did," Mac said. "And now we can go there and everything's on the up and up. So, I'll meet you there some night this week." Mac more or less saluted with his mug of coffee and winked at Elliot. "We won't have to sneak around."

"Okay," Elliot agreed loudly.

Stan leaned across the counter and took Lizzy's hand. Then he leaned in closer and attempted to kiss her.

Mac blinked as the idea touched down inside him like a burning ember. Lizzy and Stan? He shouldn't be surprised. They were both still in town, both ran businesses, had things in common. But damn, it rattled him and seemed to suck the breath right out of him. And he didn't like that he reacted to it. He planned to just be happy for them, his two old friends, together. However, he couldn't help but notice at the last moment, Lizzy avoided his kiss, and Stan's lips landed on her cheek. Her smile was still phony and forced. The cop in him took notice. Something wasn't right and whatever it was caused the coffee in his stomach to churn.

Mac didn't breathe normally until Stan was out the door and the bells were no longer jingling.

"So, Stan has lots of cats?" he asked, hoping he sounded normal and casual.

Tony topped off his coffee. "Everyone in town is starting to call him the crazy cat man. It seems like every stray in town congregates at his shop. He just feeds them all."

Working not to stare, he watched Lizzy between bites of his delicious pie and sips of coffee. She was no longer the young girl he kissed in his truck, no longer his date for the dance. She was a business-minded woman. She could kiss whomever she wanted.

It was odd the way she didn't want to kiss Stan.

Cold case or no cold case, injured leg or pain-free leg, he probably shouldn't care. He didn't care who she kissed. It had been a lifetime ago since she'd kissed *him*. She'd been a young girl. He'd been a reckless sports jock.

They weren't kids anymore. And he hadn't thought about kissing Lizzy since he graduated from college. He hadn't even thought about Lizzy at all until he thought he was dying when he'd thought about what he needed to say to her. But the cop in him took notice of things that didn't add up. It was what got the job done for him, taking those small details and putting together the puzzle that led him to solving the crime. That ability was what made him a good agent, at least until he'd gotten shot.

Forget about kissing anyone. It was a small off-kilter detail he could put the back burner right now. He had other things to think about. And whatever he knew he needed to say to her to close the door on her, he wouldn't say it now in the middle of her shop with others around to hear it.

As soon as he did, and as soon as he healed and knew where he stood with his job, and as soon as he found out all he could about the unsolved murder of Kelly Mattis, he could drive out of Mossy Point for good. Leave Lizzy to Stan's cheek kisses that shouldn't bother him. But did.

Yes, the sooner he could finish what he hoped to do and get out of town, the better.

It was probably the best thing, since he doubted after he was finished, he'd be welcomed by anyone. Least of all Lizzy.

Chapter Three

Lizzy stepped into the kitchen and put her back to the door that led out to the dining area and counter. When her parents retired to Florida and left the bakery to her, she'd had no regrets. At least she told herself she didn't. She had finished her MBA at the local university where she could commute from home and still work in the bakery when she wasn't in class. She loved the bakery. She really did.

She leaned over the huge counter, rested her chin in her palms, closed her eyes and breathed in a deep breath of the heavenly scent of yeast and bread. "I really do love the bakery." Her whispered words were met with only silence. "I really do love the bakery," she repeated.

People drove miles for her cake donuts. Brides in two counties hired her to make their wedding cakes.

The thought of that didn't seem to calm her much because then all that came out was, "Oh, God...Oh, God... Why now?"

She didn't deserve this feeling—this need for more that emerged when she saw Mac again. All she'd ever done was play by the rules. She'd not allowed herself to think about him or wonder about him in years. Now he'd waltzed into her shop as if he'd never left town. His dark honey colored hair and Paul Newman eyes demanded her attention. His easy smile had the ability to send a jolt of current right into her soul. And the way he savored each bite he took of her pie made her long to be out there at the counter feeding it to him.

"You okay?"

Antonio's voice startled her. She turned to find him standing in the doorway. He'd been out in the dining room, helping out as he did a few times a week, serving more pie to a couple when Mac walked in. "Of course I'm okay," she replied quickly.

"Oh, really? Is that why there are tears in your eyes, little sister?"

She wiped at her eyes. "It just still smells like the onions I sliced this morning for the croissant sandwiches I made for the breakfast rush, *big brother* by seven minutes. That's all."

"Right. I saw him saunter in out of the blue, like he never left. I remember when Dad forbade you to see him. How you cried every night like you thought no one would know."

"Yeah, well, I got over him a long time ago. I've grown up a little since then."

He studied her for a long moment. "Considering the way you stared at him, and the way he looked at you, and the way you avoided Stan's little kiss, I doubt that matters."

She met his dark gaze, wondering for the umpteenth time why he was still in this dinky, one-horse town. He was the twin that got the dark, Italian eyes and perfect features. He was the one everyone noticed. He had straight A's in school, acted superbly in drama club, showed true creative talent in metal shop and wood shop class, and excelled in sports. All the teachers loved him. All the girls wanted him. He could have done anything. After one semester at Mizzou—the University of Missouri, he'd chosen to come home and go with her to the community college and learn IT, which was as easy for him to learn as breathing. So, he spent his time these days—when he wasn't helping her—fixing and installing computers and security systems. He helped everyone in a fifty-mile radius set up websites and blogs and pod casts. If it involved anything technical, he was on top of it.

"I'll bet Stan doubts it, too," Tony said. "I felt your coolness toward him from across the room."

She let out a huff and covered her eyes for a moment. "Stan doesn't deserve this, either. He's been kind and patient."

"I know. Everyone around who might be remotely watching can see you've done nothing but put him off."

"He's been looking at engagement rings. He showed me pictures of five different settings and asked if I liked any of them."

Tony gave her a crooked grin. "And did you?"

"You aren't helping."

"Neither are you. If you aren't really interested, you should let him off the hook to pursue someone else."

She sighed again. "I can always depend on you to tell me exactly how things are."

He drew closer, lowering his voice. "Do you really want me to tell you how I think things are?"

She was surprised by the shift in the conversation. "Yes."

"I think you're cover for him."

For a moment, Mac being in the next room eating pie and shifting her world upside down with his return was forgotten. But only for a moment. "Cover? What kind of cover?"

"I don't know. I can't quite put my finger on it. I think Stan is just a bit *too* patient and *too* kind and a lot *OCD* when it comes to little details. He seems to like you fair enough, especially wants to kiss you if he thinks someone might be watching, but the world doesn't seem to stop when he looks at you—like it just did for you and Mac. And you've pretty much spent the past year simply sharing time with him—hem-hawing around. Anyone else would have moved on by now, like all the other guys in your life since Mac left. Mac says he's here for the reunion and the picnic celebration, but hell, he didn't even come home when his brother got married. So, I don't know if I believe that, either. Whatever his reason, I'd be willing to bet you don't have a lot of time with him. You'd better set things straight while you got the chance."

"I don't have anything to set straight with him."

"If you say so." With his loaded explanation about Stan that left more questions than answers, he headed back out to the dining area. Out the door, she saw him set more coffee to brew. Beyond him, Mac was staring at her again, watching her, studying her.

There was hunger in his eyes that he didn't begin to try and mask. He also didn't try to hide the way he more than mentally undressed her. It left her unnerved. It was as if he had the ability to peel back all the layers of her and peer into her soul.

She didn't need it. She didn't need *him*.

****

Mac left as soon as he finished his pie. It took every ounce of control he had to appear casual as he made his way out the door. And he didn't think about the catch in his leg until he lifted it to the running board to climb into his truck. He was certain if he stayed another second in the sweet-roll scented place, he was going to suffocate. Also, he needed to be alone with Lizzy. At the same time, he knew it was a bad idea. Either way, he was sure Tony wouldn't leave if he was there. He'd have to get her alone somewhere else.

What the hell was he thinking? He shouldn't get her alone.

The last thing his career or his heart needed was to be alone with Lizzy Signorino. Besides he didn't need to be alone with her to say whatever it was he needed to say. He paused, sitting in his truck. Just what did he need to say to her in order to close the door on that part of his life anyway? That he was sorry? That he wished they'd been given more time? That the night of the dance was a great little memory, but it was really swallowed by the nightmare that followed? For a moment, he couldn't remember just what it was he'd thought about when he was shot and he wanted to make sure all the T's were crossed and the I's were dotted when it came to his life. He only knew Lizzy was unfinished business. And now that he was back and she was mere yards away, he couldn't think of a single word.

As a high school jock, she'd been a conquest. As a dance date, she'd been a girl he'd wanted. He'd spent the year after his graduation missing her and wanting her. When he let it sink in he would never have her, he let her go.

And yes, he was over her.

He'd trudged away and left that young girl behind.

What he saw in the bakery was a woman, grown and all business with curves in all the right places, and lips that he remembered could kiss well. They'd been only kids, reckless kids, but Lizzy hadn't turned her cheek or avoided his kiss.

He couldn't deny the attraction that tugged at him, and it had nothing to do with the past. It was a lot like what he'd experience in his father's orchard, like that sense of finding his way home and being in a place that felt right. He should ignore it, but he found himself not wanting to. Thanks to his career, he'd left behind everything that was home and he'd forgotten how good it felt to be there. It was something he decided to consider later. Right then, his thigh burned and Lizzy's coffee felt like it spun in his stomach. He told himself she was with Stan. *Good for them*, he thought. *Have a nice life*. He had other things to think about.

He had an unsolved murder to study and a leg that needed to heal.

Maybe he didn't need to say anything at all to her. Maybe he just needed to close the imaginary Lizzy door and march away. That didn't seem too hard, despite the pain in his leg. All he needed to do was wrap himself around the cold case of Kelly Mattis, just like he put himself into every other case he worked. Once the decision was made, he let out a sigh of relief.

Coming back wasn't a mistake.

He knew no one else would have the inside advantage and be able to do the job as he thought he could. And he thought solving this unsolved crime while he healed and decided the next course of his career seemed like a good idea.

He looked down the street to City Hall and his father's previous office, wondered if his father missed it at all. He started the truck and left the rich aroma of pastry behind when he drove to the Village Park, sat on a bench, listening to birds and breathing fresh air while he read his father's first notebook.

Maybe doing his job would get his mind off the woman he just left. Maybe thinking about the case at hand would help him forget the night near the tunnel. After reading notes, he learned that not only could he not forget the night, what he needed to do was return to it. The tunnel was exactly where he needed to go.

After a short drive, he stepped into the shade of the tunnel. Mac forced away the shiver that threatened to slide up his back at what felt like a twenty-degree colder temperature drop from the sunshine he'd just left. The tunnel smelled of mold and moss and earth. As a kid, Mac had been dared to step into Marston's Tunnel. He never stepped farther than the sunlight. Until now.

Except for Kelly Mattis, obviously her murderer, and the authorities who investigated her murder, he didn't know anyone who did.

Even now, he remembered the dank, moldy smell that had touched him as he stood at the entrance as a young boy, his friends on their bikes calling him a scaredy cat, even though he knew none of them would go in either. The smell hadn't changed much.

Strangely enough, Mac thought the coppery scent of blood even burned his nose a little, as if that would still remain after almost a decade. Perhaps it had somehow absorbed into the walls. A morbid thought, he knew, but it touched him just the same and he fought down another shiver.

He thought of the killer he now hunted. "Do you ever come here?" he whispered. "Do you ever come back to visit this place? Do you spend time here, knowing you're safe because everyone else is too damned scared to step foot in this place? I'll bet you do, you son of a bitch."

The stains of Kelly Mattis's blood still decorated some of the bricks like old brown sidewalk chalk that had been partially washed away by the rain.

He closed his eyes and allowed his memories to take him back to that night. He hated that he couldn't forget that night. At the same time, he wished he could remember more—if he saw Kelly talking to anyone, if he noticed anyone watching her, if he had seen Antonio Signorino with her. Now that he thought about it, he couldn't remember Tony being at the dance at all. Then he didn't remember much beyond Lizzy. She hadn't been like the ugly duckling. It was more like she had been the invisible duckling that blossomed into an eye-catching—and heart-grabbing—swan. Her mom had taken pictures. Her dad had made him promise to keep her safe. Tony hadn't been there. Where was he? Picking up his own date? Taking pictures at his date's house? Finding out where he'd been was first on Mac's mental list of things to check out.

He opened his eyes and sighed, thinking, knowing he might never find out who made the bracelet, or how it came to be on Kelly's wrist. He didn't even know if it was put there before or after she was dead. He'd never given up on a case yet. "And I'm not giving up on you, either, Kelly." His whispered promise was swallowed by the tunnel. It wasn't that he felt he owed it to her. He didn't owe that bitch a thing. She'd threatened to demand his class ring because he didn't respond to her as they both thought he would, as he'd planned to. What a stupid jock he'd been. No, he owed it to his town. He was damned tired of the dark cloud of murder hanging over his hometown.

A noise—the snap of a snapping stick —from the mouth of the tunnel sent his hand to the butt of his Glock.

Chapter Four

Mac relaxed, seeing her small silhouette at the mouth of the tunnel against the sunset behind her.

He studied her and mentally sent the picture of her to the saved part of his mind before he stepped toward her, not too fast so as not to appear eager.

She waited and watched his every step.

When he drew closer and saw her car parked next to his truck some yards away, he said, "You shouldn't be up here alone."

"I'm not alone," Lizzy replied. "I'm with you. Are you limping?"

He gave her a narrowed look that said *you know what I mean.* "No." At least he hoped he hadn't been limping. "So, what *are* you doing up here?"

"I followed you."

And he hadn't noticed he was being followed. The idea of that settled in his gut like a giant snowball. He needed to pay better attention and stop letting the safe, hometown feeling and trips down memory lane combined with his jock stupidness fog his brain. "Why?"

"Do you want my honest answer?"

He stepped out into the warm setting sun of fall. Now he could see her features better. And, of course, he was closer to her. Her musky scent reminded him of the woods, cool and inviting. She was close enough he could touch her.

Hell, maybe he should go back into the tunnel and keep his distance. Besides, he doubted she'd let him touch her. Mac took a deep breath and tried to cool his jets. It seemed where Lizzy Signorino was concerned, he didn't have any control over his reaction. His soul, his heart, or his dick. He told himself he reacted to her this way because he hadn't had any in a long time.

"I'd expect nothing but honesty from you, Lizzy. Ever."

"I followed you up here to get some closure."

"Closure?"

The single word question popped out before he could stop it. He knew what the hell closure was. And yet he hadn't had to ask. That was what he'd decided he'd needed as two bullets burned in him. He didn't know until that moment he needed the same thing because what was lying in wait left from that wonderful, horrible night was something resembling a huge wound that could never heal no matter what he tried to slap over the top of it. He just didn't know that seeping wound existed until he thought he might die. It was worse, more painful, than his fucking leg. He'd kissed and held and touched her just a few yards from where he stood now. He was a cop who knew the rules and lived and played by them. Standing before her now with the soft breeze touch his face, he worked to keep her on the back burner.

Maybe it was the place, but right then, he didn't feel like closing any door. He wanted to kiss her. And it had nothing to do with his past. He was a grown man and knew what he wanted—the woman standing before him.

He'd want to kiss her, taste her even if he met her in a crowded room in New York City. He'd even tried to tell himself kissing her wouldn't matter. He could kiss and fuck his way all the way to Cleveland. Or Timbuktu. He hadn't. In fact, he had kissed very few women. He'd been too busy making the most of his job, and the empty feeling he'd been left with hadn't been worth it.

"Yes, closure. You never said a word to me after that night..."

"I kinda believed your dad when he said I'd better stay away and never try to talk to you again. I thought maybe he might put a hit out on me or something."

Her beautiful eyes widened. "A hit?"

"He *is* Italian."

Now she rolled her eyes at him.

"You could have at least answered one of my letters," he said. "*That might have given us both closure.*" *And we wouldn't be here wondering where we stand.*

"Letters?"

He didn't think she could fake the dumbfounded expression on her face. And he knew instantly why she never answered a letter. The girl who had stared at him with longing in her expression as her dad took her from the police station that horrible night eleven years ago, would never have not replied to his letter. Even if her father forbade her, she would have found a way.

"I never got any letters." Her voice was laced with anger.

Yes, that monster gnawed at his insides, too. He sucked in a breath and forced it to calm. After all this time, he didn't have the room or the time to waste on anger.

"I never got anything. Then I found out that you only took me to the Homecoming dance because Kyle dared you. You used me. I guess you didn't get everything you wanted from me up here at Marston's Tunnel. So, you just sauntered on to the next piece of ass willing to share it with you. For me, it wasn't so easy leave or forget."

She looked like she wanted to leave right then as she took a few steps toward the tunnel, as if all the secrets of that night were held there. Maybe they were. Yet, she faced the woods and avoided him as she spoke.

"Kelly Mattis was never my friend. She called me a geek and book worm. And little miss goody two shoes. She even once called me a fucking bore. Then she laughed and said, 'Oh, wait, you're just a bore because you aren't fucking anybody. No one's ever going to want to fuck you. You should just join a convent right now.'"

Mac digested this information by glancing up at the sky before he took in all the changing colors of the trees that surrounded them. He clenched his fists to keep from touching her as he met her gaze again.

Damn it all to hell, he hadn't known any of this. The cattiness of girls always amazed him. In his job in the past ten years, he'd learned women could be just as bad.

Before he could think of a reply, she continued. "I suppose I should thank her. Because that night up here with you, I would have let you. Hell, I wanted you to, just so I could dangle it in front of her nose and prove her wrong. Then she was dead, and I couldn't dangle anything in front of her. Not long after that I found out I was just a dare to you..."

She paused and took a breath. "Then I was expected—just expected—to take over the bakery. Don't get me wrong, I live to bake just like my dad did. But that night has hung over my head like a bad dream that never goes away. And I thought if I could just come here, to this place and tell you..."

His chest ached from her words. He'd only known his own pain, his own desire to get out of town. He'd known she kept to herself back in the day, known she was thought of as being mousy and even stuck up, but he had never really thought about how other students might have treated her. "Tell me what?"

"That I—"

"You what?"

Tears suddenly slid down her cheeks like lightning bolts. He stared at them. How was he supposed to heal or find answers and do his job when seeing a tear on her cheek felt worse than the bullet that pierced his leg? Shit, he didn't need this. He didn't need these feelings he didn't know still existed, obviously dormant in his soul.

"That I ha—" She stopped and hastily wiped the tears from her face. "God, I can't even tell you how much I hate you...I'm so stupid."

She started to turn away as if she planned to head to her car and leave. Mac grabbed her by her arm and forced her to face him. In the next heartbeat, she was in his arms, her entire body crushed against his, the side of her face against his chest where she could surely hear his heart racing. He wrapped his arms around her, feeling like things were right in the world for the first time since the first bullet slammed into his leg, feeling right and perfect like hiking through his dad's orchard.

She stood there for a moment with nothing but the sounds of her breathing mixing in with the sounds of the insects in the trees that surrounded them. Then she struggled against him. "No! No! I'm not falling for this again. I'm not—"

He refused to let her go. "It did start out as a dare. And it became so much more, something I wasn't sorry I took. I never used you. Never, Lizzy. Of that, I promise. I wish I could change that night, too, and get rid of the cloud that hangs over the town, but I can't. You say you thank Kelly. I hate her. She has invaded my life in ways you can't imagine, in ways I can't share with you. And I *did* write you letters. Starting the day after graduation. That was my closure." At least he thought it was. Apparently it hadn't been enough when bullets slammed into him.

"While we were in school that last year, I at least got to see you, got to see you as I passed you in the hall."

He chuckled bitterly. It was strange how nature around them was so normal—insects and birds chirping, when he was trying to put things into perspective and one of their classmates had died a horrid, untimely death a few yards away. "And you probably didn't know that I'd sneak a candy bar or something into your locker. After school ended, I knew I wouldn't have that anymore. So, I started the letters. Sometimes it was only one a week, other times it might be three or four that I mailed to your house. They said everything from *please write me back* to *I'm thinking about you,* to four or five pages of every single thing I did in the previous two days. It was a whole crazy journal of a year of my life, my way of summing it up. A year of hell where every day I anticipated as well as dreaded opening my mail box."

He met her gaze, her emerald eyes were shiny. He saw determination and perhaps a bit of anger etched into her expression. He forced in a breath and felt her breasts against him with the action.

Amazing, he thought. After all the time apart, his want for her was so much stronger, a thousand times stronger. Unbelievable, but so true.

If there was one thing he'd learned while his leg and side was bleeding, it was never to waste a moment. He leaned down and touched his lips to hers. Not too gently. Not forceful. Just needful. Her kiss was...good. It felt right, like being back in town, like breathing fresh, apple air.

She let out a sob that he mistook as a moan and slipped away from him before he could stop her a second time. "No..." She sounded like a wounded animal. "No, I will *not* fall for this again." She backed away from him as she spoke. "Stay away from me, and leave me alone. And stay out of my bakery."

This time he let her go, and he let her grasp the door handle of her car before he spoke. "Ask your parents about my letters, Lizzy."

She paused enough to let him know his words hit her. Then she got into her car, slammed the door, started it, and left.

Mac stood where he was for a long moment, allowing his heart to return to normal as he listened to the sounds of insects and birds in the trees.

How long he stood there, he wasn't certain.

What he was certain of was that the insects in the woods over his left shoulder grew quiet. Then he again heard the sound of a twig breaking beneath a foot. The hair on the back of his neck stood up and his breath caught as he was on instant alert, ready with his gun in his hand. He scanned the woods for several long seconds, but saw no one. He searched and waited and studied until the chirps of the crickets returned. He never relaxed.

Someone had been there.

Watching.

Someone had probably seen him with Lizzy. Shit.

Someone had seen him with his gun in his hand. Shit.

Maybe it was just a kid or a group of boys out exploring the woods, feeling courageous, getting close to Marston's Tunnel as he and his friends had done growing up.

No, he would have heard the laughter of boys if that was the case.

Chapter Five

In the loft apartment above the bakery where Lizzy now called home, she paced.

She paused only long enough to take a drink of the wine she'd poured into a tumbler because she hadn't taken the time to search out a wine glass. There were no more tears. She was too enraged to cry anyway.

Letters.

He'd written her letters. Good God, she'd gone all this time thinking he'd used her, that she was nothing more than a notch—almost—on his headboard. Now she didn't know who to be angry at more: herself or her parents. Or perhaps Tony, if he'd known about the letters, too. She no longer hated Mac.

Maybe she did hate him. For stepping back into her life, for making her want him again.

And she hadn't even gotten the chance to ask him why he was there or what he was doing in the tunnel.

Hell, she didn't know anyone who ventured into that place. Ever. Except Kelly Mattis. And whoever killed her.

Her lips still sizzled with something close to an electrical current from his kiss. The only positive thing about the day was that she'd managed to get pies and pastries ready for tomorrow before her little trek to Marston's Tunnel.

Marston's Tunnel.

She hadn't even been to that side of town since the night of the dance.

What had she been thinking?

When she spotted him driving through town near the end of the day, she'd followed him. She wasn't even sure why. It was as if he had some sort of homing device, and she was called to follow him. What was wrong with her? She wasn't some infatuated teenager anymore. She told herself she only followed him so she could tell him to go to hell and she could gain her closure. When she saw him head to Marston's Tunnel, she'd stopped some distance way and watched him go into the tunnel.

What the hell was he thinking going in there? Only murderers and victims dared to enter in there. There were probably a few ghosts, too.

Why she didn't leave, she still couldn't explain. All she knew was she had to find out why he would go into Marston's Tunnel. She'd been dumb enough to think he might want to go to the spot where they'd parked all those years ago to seek some sort of closure like she'd wanted. From where she'd watched him, he hadn't given their parking spot more than a glance before he purposefully entered the tunnel.

She should have left him there, but she found herself slightly miffed that the tunnel held more call than the place not too far away where she'd nearly handed him her virginity on a silver platter. And she'd followed him, parking next to his truck and getting out of her car.

She told herself it was to see why he was in the tunnel.

At least she tried to convince herself of that. Then she'd found she couldn't step into the tunnel. Seeing him down there where Kelly Mattis had been killed, just standing as if he searched for something left more questions. And she hadn't gained closure or learned what he was doing there.

Then their conversation hadn't been anything close to what she'd planned.

Then he kissed her.

Leaving her about as far from any kind of closure as she could possibly be.

Damn him.

Letters.

She swallowed a big gulp of her wine, felt it slide down to her stomach, felt a hint of warm come with it. Then the warmth was gone as if it couldn't penetrate the cold emptiness that filled her.

She'd waited long enough. The anger and the emptiness weren't going to be washed down with any amount of wine. Grabbing her phone from the nearby counter, she dialed her mom in Florida. It was an hour later in Florida, but she didn't care. Her parents no longer had to go to bed early—like she now did—in order to get up to have the bakery ready.

"Mom?"

"Hi, honey." When Lizzy said nothing, her mother went on. "Is everything all right?"

"No—yes. Everything's fine." It felt like the biggest lie she'd ever told her mother. "I called because I have to ask you..."

"I already know what this is about."

"You do?" That would certainly make this easier, Lizzy thought.

"Yes, Antonio called me and let me know that Mac—James McLane— was back in town."

"He did?"

"Yes. And Lizzy, I know how you've pined for him."

"I haven't pined for him. Only young, naive girls pine for guys." She refused to be one of those.

"I know how you've never really gotten over him, never let anyone else even close to your heart."

Maybe this wasn't going to be easy. "How could you possibly know? I..." Lizzy thought she'd done a good job burying her true feelings, hiding them even from herself, and keeping herself numb for so long it was hard to feel anything while she always forced a smile on her face. Lizzy herself hadn't even known how far from being over Mac she was until he'd stepped into her bakery today.

"A mother knows. A mother feels what her children feel. Someday you'll know."

Not at this rate, Lizzy thought. There wasn't anyone she thought qualified to be the father of any children she might produce. Except Mac.

She cut that thought off with a sudden, sharp, mental sword. The very last thing she needed was to think about any children and Mac in the same thought wavelength. She needed to get back to the subject at hand quick, before she managed to think any other stupid, useless thoughts.

"He said he wrote me letters, Mama."

Her mother was quiet, confirming the truth with her silence.

Lizzy felt deflated as well as defeated as she let her breath out in a whoosh. "Oh, Mom..."

"At the time, it seemed like the right thing to do, Liz. That young man had taken you out somewhere with the plans to have his way with you. This, I might add, in the eyes of a parent, is a very dangerous thing. And he placed you in an even more dangerous place, just a few yards from a murder. What would you expect? Your father and I only wanted to protect you and keep you safe. It's what parents do. Protect their children."

"I know that. Mom, we're talking a *lot* of letters here."

"Yes, I know. I had to switch boxes to something bigger three times."

Bloody hell. "This is my life, Mom."

"Yes, and I'm so sorry, my darling. You don't know how many times I wanted to tell you. At first, I considered just throwing them away when they arrived. Yet that didn't seem like the right thing to do. Then, as time went on, it got harder and harder to tell you. And you were in college, making new friends. You were seeing that young man. What was his name? Eric?"

It was a good thing her mother remembered, because Lizzy would have had to think about it for a while, which was a clear indication as to how much of a lasting impression the guy made on her.

"And we thought you were over that time of your life. After all, you were so busy with school and the bakery. You spent every moment learning everything your father and I knew about pastries and pies and bread and the perfect cake icing. And then the letters stopped. To tell you the truth, I kind of forgot about them until today when your brother called."

Lizzy closed her eyes, feeling as if someone just socked her in the stomach. *Forgot.* If only she had been able to forget so easily. She'd poured her soul and her energy into work and class in order to forget. And she had forgotten with time. Until today when he stepped into her bakery. Until he kissed her. If she didn't know better, she'd think he sucked her brain out with that kiss. Then everything she thought she'd managed to forget shot down through her like a bolt of lightning. Now she had to work to find her voice. "Where are they, Mom?"

If her mother said they were destroyed, Lizzy would be destroyed too. "They are in the storage locker where your dad put all the old equipment he was afraid to get rid of. They're in a box labeled papers."

She let out a breath of relief. "I'll talk to you again tomorrow, Mom."

"Lizzy—"

"I love you, Mom." She hung up on her mom before she could say another word.

The air smelled of rain, and it made her quicken her steps. It was bad enough she was retrieving letters she didn't know until now even existed. She didn't need them to be soggy and ink smeared, too. In the night breeze, minus the sun, the damp air sent shivers through her as she rushed to her car. Maybe she should leave them be, leave the past where it was—in the past. All this time, she'd thought he used her. The truth was in his letters. And she deserved to know the truth.

Chapter Six

The town was filled with an array of lights. From this point of view, it looked like Christmas.

"This is still such a fun i-i-idea," Elliot said.

"Yes, it is," Mac agreed. He hadn't really planned to climb the water tower. And he wasn't really working undercover, just searching for answers. Yet, he knew digging for answers usually meant doing whatever he might do if he wasn't. This gave him such a vantage point.

His leg did the climb okay. It wasn't a hundred percent, probably wasn't even close to eighty percent, but no one saw his need to pause, either. And he hadn't realized until he sat down on the narrow catwalk at the top, hung his arms over the single-cable meant to be a railing, and took in his town from this vantage point just how much he'd missed this. People driving, people moving, a woman with a baby stroller, Mrs. Strayton still—after ten years—walking her dog. Oh, wait, it was a different dog, he noticed. Even from this height in the dusk, he could see it was a lighter colored animal than what he remembered.

Down the street, a girl decorated the inside of the window of the pharmacy with pumpkins, and orange and purple lights, and Halloween decorations. Halloween? He thought *hell, we aren't even to the middle of September yet*. On the next block, a guy changed letters on the sign of the fast-food place, advertising *Coffee $1 Every Day*. The coffee may be cheap, but he knew the place had nothing on Lizzy's apple pie. On the next block, smokers congregated out the front door of the Streetside Bar, their lit cigarettes flickering through the dusk like red Christmas tree lights as they puffed.

Elliot sat on his left. Kyle Broden, another former high school football jock, was on his right. Then was Gary Fullerman, and Tony took up space on the end.

"Too bad Jake is on patrol," Gary said, "and he can't be up here with us."

"I don't think he's on patrol," Kyle replied. "I think he's on a coffee break, given he's down there where he can get coffee for a dollar every day. Besides, I think he's put on a few more pounds than the rest of us. He might not be able to climb the ladder."

A few chuckles filled the evening.

Mac followed his gaze and saw the patrol car parked in the fast-food parking lot.

"Do you think they even ch-charge him?" Elliot asked.

"It's hard to say." Tony's voice was filled with humor but patience.

Several moments past and were filled with idle chit-chat and typical catching up. Mac saw Stan climbing the ladder to them.

"Where have you been?" Elliot asked when Stan finally sat down with them.

He wasn't quite huffing, but the climb was a workout for him. "I had some last-minute things to do at the shop."

"You did?" his brother asked. "You must have been doing them in the dark, because the shop was closed and dark when I walked past to come here."

"Forget it, Elliot."

Mac couldn't help but notice the unusual irritation and impatience in Stan's voice.

They were all quiet for a few minutes as each took in the town below them.

"What's up with you, Mac? You've been awfully quiet all night," Kyle noticed. "No cat calls, hardly any reminiscing. You haven't even asked too many questions about the reunion. And just where in the hell have you been for the last decade? It's like you fell off the face of the earth."

Mac supposed Kyle was being polite, shifting the attention and changing the subject considering Elliot frowned like he might cry for a moment. Mac followed along with it, as he figured it was as good a time as any to pick his old friends' brains. "I just wanted to get as far away from Kelly Mattis's murder as I could get. You guys know in a few days, it'll be exactly eleven years."

Again, they were all quiet, leaving Mac to think perhaps he should have waited a few days to say anything.

"Damn, Mac, what'd you have to go and talk about that for?" Kyle asked. "I don't need to be reminded of that time."

"Why not?" the question popped out before Mac thought to stop it.

"Because that was a black spot in my entire senior year, that's why."

That was an understatement, Mac thought as he remembered senior year. Now that he was on subject, he might as well see it through. "How so?"

"I used to take Torrie Aimes up to the tunnel almost every weekend that summer before our senior year. After that, she didn't let me take her anywhere."

"You were doing Torrie Aimes?" Stan asked. "I don't even remember you hanging out with her."

"Woooieeee," Elliot let out with a laugh. He seemed to easily swing to a happy side after Stan's reprimand. Maybe they just needed a completely different subject.

"Hell, only once. All the other times it was just a lot of other stuff. Took me all summer to get around the bases with her. As soon as I did, she started bossing me around and insisted I get a suit for the dance. Then that thing with Kelly happened. After that, it all fizzled out real fast. And, as I remember it, I think there were a lot of girls who weren't going out at all. They were all staying at home, or having parties at home. It seemed like every girl in town was on the buddy system after that and taking self-defense classes. Hell, everyone—not just the girls—was scared and apprehensive. What do you think, Mac? I mean, you kind of made the gruesome discovery. Doesn't it bother you that you and Lizzy were that close? Why do you even want to think about it?"

"I try not to," was all Mac could say. It was another understatement. It wasn't a lie by any means. He wished he could forget it and not have to think about it all.

It probably haunted all of them.

"Too bad Stuey Reynolds isn't in town—yet," Gary said. "We'd have most of the starting lineup for our senior football team here."

They all let out their own chuckles. And the new subject was a good change. Mac was going to have to be more subtle, he supposed. More than a decade may have passed, but the black cloud, the fear, and uncertainty hadn't faded. And, of course, questions hung in the air like a dense fog. Were they questions where no one knew the answers, or was everyone just afraid to answer them?

"Stuey's coming, isn't he?" Mac asked.

"He said he was," Gary replied.

"Before the weekend of the reunion is over and everyone leaves, we need to come back up here, hold our own reunion here," Stan suggested. "In fact, why don't we make this a planned event? Every year, or every five years, we meet again and climb up here. Let's just plan it."

Kyle agreed. "Yeah, I forgot how much we used to come up here. Why did we ever give it up?"

Mac shrugged. "We all chose a different path, that's all."

"Stan and I didn't," Elliot said.

Mac gave him a grin through the dark. "You and Stan are special." Everyone in town knew Elliot was special. "You stayed to keep an eye on the town and make sure everyone was safe."

Elliot laughed heartily. "No, we didn't. We stayed because Dad skipped town, and Stan took over the shop. Besides, Stan lost his football scholarship when he hurt his knee right after that."

"You eat like a pig. Someone had to work to pay to feed you," Stan said, his voice filled with laughter.

Mac knew it wasn't funny, knew that it bruised Stan's ego, even though Stan laughed along with his brother. Hell, it probably burned a hole that never healed in that ego. While Stan's dad's body shop paid the bills and put bread on the table when they were kids, Mac knew—just as the entire football team knew—there was more going on in that household than what the world saw.

It was no secret Stan's dad spent more than a few nights drying out in a cell at the police station before he packed up and left in the middle of the night. It was also no secret that Stan, his brother, and their mother at one time or another, had to cover bruises they sustained when Mac's dad didn't get the handcuffs on Randy Gresden quick enough. He also knew that scholarship had been Stan's ticket out of town, a ticket that had blown away in the wind in the form of a knee injury that happened at practice just after the old man skipped town. It had to bite, especially after Randy somehow got his own ticket out of town. There were rumors he took up residence in Florida or California and found himself a new woman to slam around. Mac thought that had to bite, too, like he got a new start on life when Stan, his brother, and his mom stayed here.

"You know," Stan said, "that old injury was a blessing in disguise."

"How so?" Mac asked without thinking.

"You guys all know I could never leave Elliot in the house with my dad, anyway. No matter how much he and my mom said to go."

"Yes, you could," Elliot argued, again sounding almost as if he might cry through his stutters. "We did tell you. I even said I'd help you pack. Don't blame this on me. I can take care of myself. Besides, right before you hurt your knee, Dad left. And Mom got her teaching certificate." Elliot's mood swung back to the sad side again. His voice was so filled with emotion, he stuttered every other word.

"I know you can take care of yourself, buddy," Stan said, speaking with patience like he usually did—the patience Mac recognized. "Besides, if I had gone, I might never have come back. I wouldn't be where I am now. I own the shop. I like the work, and it does well—with Elliot's help."

"I sweep the floors every day," Elliot put in, his happy outlook returning.

"Yes, and you do a great job of it."

"You wouldn't believe how messy Stan makes the floors even though everything else and all the tools have to stay in the places where they belong," Elliot said. "Still, he's a greasy slob when it comes to the floor."

"I'll bet," Mac said.

"He was that way in the locker room as I recall. Always hanging his clothes in a certain order in his locker," Kyle put in.

They all chuckled again. Mac smiled at the sibling and friend banter, for the moment missing home, missing his own brother, Gabe. He planned to spend some time with Gabe while he was here. It had taken a while for all of them to fall back into the groove, but he knew his friends. He knew with a little more time, they'd be talking locker room talk. Taking in the scene before him, his home town, the lights, the few people below him milling about, he wondered why some people—even him—were so eager to escape this. It was home. It welcomed him as no other place really did. Hell, if he listened hard enough, he thought he could hear it calling to him.

"I wouldn't be with Lizzy."

Stan's words grabbed Mac, caused his breath to catch in his chest. At the same time, the cop in him rose to the surface. There was just something in the lame way Stan spoke them, as if having Lizzy was nothing more than an afterthought, or something he didn't necessarily want, or perhaps it was as if he needed to say it so others believed it. Mac couldn't put his finger on it. He just recognized the words were a bit off kilter. He glanced down to the end and met Tony's gaze.

"You're quiet tonight, too, Tony," Kyle said.

"I'm just listening to all of you. It's nice to hear so many familiar voices. Before the week's over, we should go to the school field, climb the fence, and toss a football around. Make it really like old times."

"I'm in," Kyle said.

"Me too," Mac added.

"Count me in," said Gary.

"And me," Stan added.

"I don't know, Stan, you're fatter than you were in high school," Elliot said. "You probably can't climb the fence. I can bring some water."

"Hey, I managed to climb the ladder all the way up here, didn't I?" Stan protested.

They all laughed lightly. "I think all of us except for maybe Tony, are carrying around some extra baggage," Mac noticed.

"Speak for yourself," Gary insisted.

"Speaking of Lizzy," Kyle changed the subject, "isn't that her car down there parked at Kennedy's Storage Units?"

"It looks like it," Stan put in.

Kennedy's Storage Units were lit up like an airport runway, obviously to ward off any intruders, although Mac wasn't so certain that would be a problem in Mossy Point. From where he sat, he watched Lizzy, her hair shining under all the lights, exit one of the units. She set a box on the ground next to the door before she slid the door down closed. From this distance, Mac couldn't see exactly what she did for the next several seconds, but intuition told him she was replacing a lock before she stooped and picked up the box and carried it to her car.

"What do you think she's getting?" Elliot asked.

"Probably something she needs at the bakery. Her dad keeps a lot of bakery stuff and equipment in the storage," Stan answered. "Right, Tony?"

"Right."

Mac didn't speak, didn't trust himself to even open his mouth. He again met Tony's gaze. He saw knowledge in Tony's expression. Tony knew as well as Mac knew what she carried to her car and placed on the front passenger seat.

His letters.

His mouth was suddenly dry.

Considering the way she tried to tell him she hated him, he was surprised she didn't forget his letters as easily as she'd escaped him up by the tunnel. Then maybe she was getting them in order use them to start the bonfire Friday night that starts off the picnic.

He shouldn't want her. He shouldn't care what she did with his letters. They were old news anyway.

Or were they?

Thunder rumbled in the distance, as if in warning telling him not to go there.

He drew in a deep breath and tried to squelch any thoughts of Lizzy. It was an impossible task considering all he had to do was look down and see her. He watched her leave the storage units and drive back in the direction of the bakery where her apartment was upstairs. He saw a group of kids in the high school parking lot. He saw a herd of what were obviously very little kids working to learn and play soccer in a small open area of the park, trying to get their practice in before dark settled in completely.

The thought of Lizzy lingered.

He saw Stan and Elliot's mom, Kathleen, exit one of the storage units where Lizzy had just left. The one she'd just closed and locked was on the other side, a unit that cost extra because it provided electric.

From up here, his world was clearer.

He felt like he could see forever. He just wished he could see answers to all the questions that plagued him. He wished he didn't want Lizzy. His pants grew tight just thinking about her.

Chapter Seven

Patrolman Jake Swornson finished his coffee and gazed around the fast-food joint. He put off getting a hamburger since he'd already had one earlier in his shift for supper. He needed to cut back somewhere, and late-night burgers were a start. The smell of grease, hamburgers, and French fries hung heavy in the air and was doing battle with the scent of whatever disinfectant cleaner was now being used to clean the floor. There were plenty of cars waiting in the drive-thru, but the dining room of his favorite quick eatery was empty. Just the way he liked it this time of the night. He glanced at his phone. Eleven fifty-five. He had five minutes left of his shift. And the drive-thru had five minutes left, too, until the lights of the menu speaker would go dark. Perfect.

He needed desperately to end his shift. He'd seen motion from a distance at the ladder of the water tower. Just as he knew his former classmates were in town for the upcoming reunion, he suspected his former teammates were having their own reunion on the water tower. And because he had to work, he was stuck patrolling this one-horse town instead of enjoying some time reminiscing with his old buddies. The idea left of a sour taste in his mouth, and it had taken all his will power not to head out that direction and slap them all with a bit of a fine for leaving him out.

The sight of Sally Hillsborough as she mopped the floor helped ease the resentment. He swallowed the last gulp of his coffee and burned his throat. He sucked in a deep breath and let the bitterness slide away as he stared at Sally. It was also perfect watching her sweet ass sway back and forth with the motion.

Miranda Gray was back at the fryer, trying to finish up the few hamburgers of the drive-thru line. Sally was new, had only started recently. Until she'd started, Miranda always mopped. Jake liked watching Sally better. She had really great tits for a young girl and her entire body swayed with a rhythm that would bring Mikhail Baryshnikov to tears.

Ellen House was working in the drive-thru window. Ellen wasn't the prettiest by far. She was a little mousy and timid. Damn, though, she could suck the bottle top off a beer bottle. In fact, he had yet to find anyone who could beat her when it came to a blow job.

He was pretty certain he was in the mood for Sally. He'd yet to experience her and needed to know where she ranked with the others. The sweet sashay of her hips as she mopped told him exactly how well she could ride him.

And that was what he was in the mood for. Besides, she didn't show any contempt or disdain when she glanced his way. At least not yet. Perhaps the others had listened and heeded his threats and kept their mouths shut, and she didn't know his ways. He was, after all, protecting them. They should be grateful.

Leisurely, he got up, hoisted up his gun belt and pants and sauntered toward the door where he threw his empty cup into the receptacle before he headed out to the patrol car. Damn, he loved his patrol car. No one else in town had a computer in his car. It relayed his importance. He was a figure of authority in Mossy Point. No doubt about that. It was his job to protect everyone in town. It was the job of every resident to respect him. Pure and simple.

He climbed in, started it, and revved it a little, but not a lot to draw too much attention. Then he left the parking lot. He knew where Sally lived. He knew a convenient little spot between here and there. All he had to do was wait. He glanced at the digital clock. Eleven fifty-eight. He wouldn't have to wait long. Anticipation touched him like a caress of fingertips sliding up his arms and making the hair there stand up. His heart was already beating fast in his chest. He sucked in a deep breath and forced himself to calm. It would be pointless if he shot his wad early and alone.

After twenty-one agonizing minutes, he'd just about given up on Sally. Maybe those other two bitches told her about him and told her to take a different way home. She could always have gone Cemetery Lane, even though it would add time to her drive. Everyone knew there were less deer out that way to race out in front of you, so perhaps her parents had told her to go that way late at night. Hell, maybe her register didn't balance and she was still sniffing grease fumes trying to work it out. After all, she was new and not the brightest bulb in the closet.

Then he saw headlights.

He let out his breath, unaware he'd been holding it. She drove past him. He doubted she even noticed him.

Patrolman Swornson pulled out behind her on the narrow road and flipped on his lights, which lit up the darkness like a disco ball with an array of red and blue. No siren. He didn't think he'd need one. She was young, a new driver on the road. The lights behind her would be enough to scare her. He had his plan down pat. Calm her initial scare. Then tell her she was, indeed, speeding—even though he was pretty certain she wasn't. He didn't have a radar gun to tell her the exact speed. It didn't matter. That would raise her scare factor again. She wouldn't want a ticket. Her parents were probably paying for her little used car. She was probably spending nights flipping burgers to pay the insurance. She'd do whatever he said.

Her flashers came on. She obviously saw him behind her. She didn't slow down or move to the shoulder of the road. Not yet. What the hell was she waiting for? The grass was cut and soft, it would be a perfect place to take a little ride. Rain was holding off for now, but it would come soon, and the last thing he needed was to get his rocks off in the rain. He hated a wet uniform.

She didn't stop. She slowed and kept driving. What the fuck?

He kept following.

Anger heated through his blood and mixed with the need and anticipation that already flowed freely there. Perhaps she simply planned to pull over under a street light. Others did. The light didn't bother him, didn't worry him in the least. He knew how to work fast; he knew how to stay hidden behind the car and still get her to give him what he wanted—what he *needed*.

She didn't stop under the next street light. Between his rage, his need, his anticipation, his hard on, he felt like he might explode. He slammed his hand against the wheel. "Pull over, Sally!" He decided then he was going to make her hurt, maybe not a lot. He'd show the little bitch who was boss.

She drove slowly, three miles under the posted speed limit, not that he was really paying attention. He just thought if she drove much farther without stopping, he would make her do more than fuck him and he *would* give her a ticket. This was becoming ridiculous.

She went left at the next cross street. He followed, his rage now clouding everything. The anger boiled through him like lava, taking his need for sex to the stars. He forced in a few breaths, knowing he needed to calm down. He couldn't hurt her, couldn't leave a mark on her. No one had ever crossed the line with him like this. They all did as he expected—as his uniform required. And only once did one take the ticket instead of giving him head as he'd requested. She'd been a well-known loose woman who frequented Timbo's Tavern where she could get a cheap high. So, when she'd reported his request, he'd merely been given a 'strict' talking to by the Chief. No big deal. After all, he was working an extra twelve, sometimes two, every week because the department was so shorthanded. They needed him.

So why wasn't she stopping? He felt the muscles of his neck, tight, almost painful. And he gripped the steering wheel so tight his hands appeared white in the green glow of the dash and the red and blue spots that shined through the windshield from the lights on top of his cruiser.

Oh, when he got his hands on her...

He noticed for the first time they drove among trees, branches over the narrow lane covered them. Then she stopped in an open area. And he recognized for the first time where she'd led him. He'd been so keyed up with what he planned to do with her, he hadn't really paid attention to where he was.

"Oh, shit..."

****

Mac drove the lane to the orchard, fighting the urge to turn around and find Lizzy. All this time he'd planned to close the door on that part of his life. Close the door and let her go. He could go back to doing his job and never thinking about her at all like he'd done for perhaps the last eight years or so. It seemed like since he'd kissed her again, or since he'd met her gaze in her bakery, or perhaps since the first bullet slammed into this thigh, she'd been reeling him in like a fish caught on a line.

No, he wouldn't go to her apartment above the bakery. No, he wouldn't. He didn't want to see her with his letters. He didn't want to read them with her, hash over his own words from the past. They should leave the past buried. Now he couldn't seem to take a step forward, either.

The rain that threatened and sent him and his friends down from the water tower in a hurry turned out to be just enough drops to smear on his windshield.

Then when he saw blue and red lights reflecting off the trees of the lane, he didn't quite forget about Lizzy, but his worry jumped a hundred-fold on the worry meter as he raced the few yards around the bend to his parents' house in the orchard. A police cruiser was parked, lights flashing, behind a little blue Ford Focus.

Jake Swornson climbed out of the cruiser just as Mac stopped alongside him and killed the ignition. His worry deflated like a blown-up balloon released into a room when he saw his parents both standing on the front porch, appearing fine, although sharing his worried expression. Ozzie, the golden retriever, sat at attention obediently next to Mac's dad. He climbed out. "Dad?"

His dad held up a hand and stepped down from the porch. Ozzie followed, but obeyed Robert's motion command to sit. "Everything's fine, son." Then his dad turned his attention to the Focus. "You can get out, Sally."

Sally, his cousin, whom he hadn't seen since she was probably five or six, but whom he recognized immediately because her face hadn't changed much, climbed out from behind the wheel and rushed to his father. She still resembled his Aunt Dorothy. Ozzie still sat, but scooted closer so he could sniff Sally.

His dad gathered her into something close to a hug while still managing to face Jake Swornson.

Jake had packed on perhaps twenty-five pounds since high school, and it wasn't muscle. He tugged on his pants, hiking them up as he climbed out of the car. His face was pudgy, jowls where there hadn't been any at the bottom of his football helmet back in high school. He had lost that 'I'm a football jock' look. Mac was willing to bet none of the previous cheerleaders showed him much attention these days. And Mac was pretty certain he wouldn't have been able to climb to the top of the water tower with him and the others earlier that evening.

"Would you care to explain what this is about, Officer Swornson?"

Mac recognized his father's tone of voice. He was again the Chief of Police, or at least a man whose authority no one questioned. Mac imagined his father would be on his deathbed and still manage to have that don't-mess-with-me-and-give-me-a-solid-answer tone. Mac gave his healing thigh an absent rub before stepping over next to his father, Sally and Ozzie between them, his mom still on the porch.

"Sir, I put on my lights to pull her over, but she never did."

"She didn't have to pull over until she reached a public or familiar place, and when she got her license, I gave her instructions to come here. So, she called me to tell me she was coming here."

"I see. She used her cell phone? Driving while talking on a phone is illegal in this state."

"I have Bluetooth. I didn't touch my phone," Sally interceded.

"Why were you pulling her over?" Robert asked.

"Speeding," Swornson said.

"I wasn't—"

Mac's father shushed her. "And what did you clock her doing? I'd like to see the number on the radar gun, please."

"I don't have that anymore."

Mac glanced at his dad to see Robert's brows raise in question that. "You don't have it anymore?" Robert asked.

"No, sir."

"I suggest we let this go, then."

This was a first for Mac. His dad didn't *let things go*. Had never *let things go*.

"After all, I doubt you want to waste your time trying to write a ticket when you don't have an exact number for the speed at which she was traveling, right?"

Jake Swornson stared at them for a long moment. Mac wondered again just what the hell was going on here. Then the officer shrugged. "I suppose that would be best." His attention moved to Sally. "Drive safe going home. Keep it under the speed limit." In the bright lights of the headlights, he met Mac's gaze. "Nice to see you, Mac. We'll have to get together for a drink or two before the reunion this week."

Mac nodded. "That sounds like a good plan." Something in his gut told him it wasn't going to happen, though.

Sally said nothing, but Mac noticed his dad tightened the arm he held around the girl.

"We'll see that my niece gets home safely," Robert said.

Mac saw a flash of surprise in Jake's eyes. It was quick, but it was there. He didn't know Sally was related to the former Chief of Police. With a nod, a smile that appeared forced and, "Chief," he offered as a good night send off, Jake opened the driver's door of his cruiser and got in. He started it. The flashing red and blue lights went off as he drove out of the orchard. There were only the sounds of his tires crunching on the gravel. Within seconds, that faded into the night and was replaced by the songs of crickets.

Then his dad let out a heavy sigh, and Sally burst into tears.

"I wasn't speeding," she said through sobs.

"It's okay," Robert assured her. "What were you doing driving out so late on a school night?"

"I was driving home from work."

Mac swallowed hard. He felt like the big brother protector here. No one made his little cousin cry. No one picked on anyone in his family. Ever. He might have a few words for Jake next time they were eye to eye.

Robert smiled at her. "Oh, that's right. Your dad told me you started flipping hamburgers."

She grinned through subsiding sobs, tears shiny on her cheeks in the glow of the porch light. "My parents..."

"Are on their way," his mom said from behind them.

"Oh, Aunt Ginna, no..." She slipped out of Robert's embrace.

"It's okay, honey. They aren't mad. You did the right thing. They're just glad you're here and safe." Ginna hurried down off the porch and put an arm across the girl's shoulders. "Let's go inside and wait. I'll make you some cocoa."

"But..."

"But nothing, everything's fine. You're fine and you're safe."

"And," Robert continued, "why don't you give up your job at the burger joint? Then you don't have to work until midnight."

Together, they started heading into the house, up the steps and onto the porch. Ozzie's tail swished against Mac's legs.

"I can't do that," Sally insisted. "I need the money to pay my insurance."

"You could come here and work in the orchard. I'll pay you, and you'll only have to work daylight hours." Before she might argue more, Mac's dad continued. "At least tell me you'll think about it. And talk it over with your parents."

"Okay."

"Besides, smelling like apples and outdoors has to be better than smelling like a French fry," Mac teased her. "Unless, of course, you want me to start calling you small fry."

She chuckled and gave him a half-hearted hug, "Oh, James, it's good to see you."

"It's good to see you, too, squirt." He smiled at his mom. "I think we could all use some cocoa."

Ginna and Sally disappeared into the kitchen. Mac touched his dad's arm and kept him outside. "Care to tell me what just happened?"

"Something I'd heard as a rumor, but that I hoped it wasn't true."

"Oh?" he said softly so his cousin couldn't hear from the kitchen in case the door wasn't completely closed.

His dad back stepped onto the porch and allowed the screen door to close. "I heard one of the officers in the department was demanding sexual favors in lieu of tickets. I couldn't believe it. That shit would have never happened when I was in charge. Daniels is scared of being shorthanded, he's scared people might side with the officer, divide the town and make bigger problems. At least I think that's the reason he does nothing. Then again, I thought he did nothing because these were just that—rumors."

"And then you did what?" Mac asked, knowing full well the steps his father probably took.

"I told Sally and all your cousins, as well as your aunts and your mom, to not stop if they saw flashing lights behind them. I told them to come here. The law states you now don't have to pull over right away but can drive with flashers on to the police station or to a public place." Robert shook his head as he spoke, as if it was hard to face, much less believe it could happen in his town. Then he let out a heavy, painful sigh.

Mac knew his dad would always think of this as his town. "It sounds to me that he's not even trading sex for tickets if the girl isn't speeding." Saying it left a sour taste in his mouth was a huge understatement.

He leaned against the rail of the porch and stared out at the yard and part of the orchard through the darkness as he tried to remember Jake in high school. He knew him on the playing field, but he didn't hang out with him and never really knew how he treated members of the opposite sex. Maybe he needed to investigate that.

He'd come to heal, to see which direction he should go, spend his time trying to solve a cold case, or at least make some headway in it. It appeared he had his work cut out for him if he was going to clean up a few other things in town. Because this was his town, and like his dad, he thought of it as such. Also like his dad, he could never turn his back on something wrong. He thought of his sweet cousin as a little girl. He remembered helping her get a hot dog at a cook out more than ten years ago.

And he'd be damned if he could ignore this or pretend it didn't happen.

Chapter Eight

In the early gray light of dawn, Lizzy sat cross legged beside the counter in the bakery, the box of letters open and many of them scattered around her like fallen leaves. A butter knife, which she'd used as an envelope opener, rested on the floor near her knee.

She hadn't taken them up to her apartment. She'd thought it might be easier to read them down here, in this public place that comforted her in its rich scent of yeast and bread and apple fritters. That wasn't the case. She was pretty sure there was no place on earth that might make it easy to read them. Except perhaps up near Marston's Tunnel with Mac there to hold her and read them to her like the poet he obviously was. His written words ripped out her heart. Time and time again, she blinked back tears as she read them. She refused to cry. She'd shed enough tears over James McLane. Now, she held one hugged to her chest and breathed as those tears threatened to spill over to her cheeks.

Please. I need you.

Just four words, but they had the power to touch her soul. Mac's last letter, according to the postmark.

She understood the why—her parents wanted her safe. What she didn't understand was the how. How had they managed to keep these from her? How had she missed this? She'd poured her attention into the bakery and to college, that's how. He'd pined for her for a year, then he'd obviously found something more appealing than pouring out his life's story to her by the way of letters.

She closed her eyes and took a deep breath. The pain in her chest was so real, so deep, deeper than it had been even all those years ago when her father had come to fetch her at the police station.

"So, you found them?"

Tony's voice startled her, made her gasp, though it sounded more like a sob.

She met his dark gaze. "You knew about them, too?" She was closer to him than she was to any other person, and his knowing and keeping them from her cut another slice through her tortured heart.

He shrugged and sat down cross legged next to her. "I stumbled across them by accident when I retrieved something from the storage unit about two years ago."

"You didn't think they might be something I'd want to know about? Or need to know about?"

He sighed heavily. "Years had passed. I didn't think you'd still care."

"I didn't. It was all so long ago. Now after reading his words, it feels like yesterday somehow."

"Yeah." He dragged out the word before he took her hand. 'What do you think he's back in town for, anyway?"

It was her turn to shrug. "Closure, maybe."

After he'd kissed her up by the tunnel, she doubted if he was here for closure. If he were, he wouldn't have admitted writing letters. That was more like opening up old wounds, not closing them. At the same time, why the hell would he want to venture into Marston's Tunnel? That made no sense at all. She didn't share that part with her brother, or she'd have to share why she'd followed Mac there.

She wiped her fingers against her cheek and discovered a tear or two had managed to escape her eyes. She still held the open letter. "Hell, maybe he's just here for a picnic and a reunion."

"Yeah, maybe."

"This is where he grew up. This is where his family lives. That's all the reason he really needs, right?"

"Right. So, what are you going to do, little sister?"

"I should try to avoid him," she replied, even though she was certain—especially after reading a few of what had to be a couple hundred letters—it wouldn't be possible.

Tony gave her hand a squeeze. "I'm not talking about Mac. I'm talking about Stan."

"Oh..." It sounded more like a moan, as if she suddenly remembered he still existed. "I'm letting him off the hook today. We make great friends, but I know now we can never be more than that. The chemistry just isn't there. The spark..."

"Like the spark I saw when Mac shuffled in?"

Hesitantly, she folded up the letter she held and placed it carefully back into the envelope where it had remained for a decade. She was hesitant to put any of them back into their respective envelopes. For some stupid, immature reason she couldn't push aside, she wanted to stack them up in order and read his words every day. She didn't share those thoughts with her brother, but she had the feeling he'd somehow know. "How do I put out that spark? Especially when it's more like a bonfire. Or maybe even an explosion."

Yes, Tony did know her. "Do you really want to?"

"Am I wrong to say no?"

He shook his head. "I think everyone deserves to have what they want—sometime in their life."

He spoke as if there was something he wanted he thought he could never have, but she couldn't dwell on it just then. Not with Mac tugging at her soul in the form of old letters. "Even if it disrupts the lives of others? I mean let's face it, I doubt Daddy will be happy if I tell him Mac's back."

"Dad's not here. And you're not seventeen anymore."

"I've worked so hard to make this into more than just a bakery."

He chuckled. "Oh, don't I know it. You've done little *but* work. I think you've worked hard enough to open five bakeries, and I think you did it to put Mac behind you, or maybe just that night." He looked around. "And you've turned this into a great place. Did you ever think it might be time for a vacation? Besides, what does working the bakery have to do with following your heart and pouring your feelings out to Mac?"

"Why am I even talking about this? Why would I think I should pour my feelings out to Mac? It's been ten long years. We've both gone our own direction. Why would we go back? He's probably not interested." Again, the idea of his kiss fluttered through her thoughts. That kiss told her he was definitely interested.

Tony looked right at her, hard. "I'm not talking about going back. I'm talking about stepping forward. I think you've been stalled long enough. I bet the day's bakery receipts he is interested."

"How would you know?"

He grinned that grin she knew melted women's hearts. "I work IT. I know everything. About everybody. And I'm not blind, deaf, or stupid. I saw the way he stared at you today when he saw you. And I just saw the way he watched you from the top of the water tower where we were all sitting."

"You climbed the water tower?"

"Yep."

"Don't let Mom know."

He still grinned. "She never knew about all the other times I climbed it."

She studied him for a long moment. "So, what do you know? About Mac?"

"I know where he's been for the last decade."

"How? Because you searched his name on your computer?" Lizzy could have done that. She never had. It would be more painful to know about him than to not know about him. At least that was what she continued to tell herself. She knew for certain she didn't want to see him with a pretty wife and a couple of kids who shared his blue eyes.

"No, I know all about Mac because he wrote letters to me, too, and emails. Only I wrote him back."

****

Deep into the night, Mac pored over his father's notebook, reading and re-reading Robert's journal entries and notes and thoughts until the words blurred and a headache settled behind his eyes. Absently, he rubbed the bridge of his nose. The small lamp on the night stand was bright enough, but he was tired. It was exhausting just trying to concentrate when Lizzy and Sally filled his thoughts. He considered turning it off and simply sleeping among the notes, open files, and his dad's notebook.

His dad and officers of the Major Case Squad had questioned almost everyone in the high school, students and faculty, himself included. The only thing that had been determined was that Kelly Mattis was promiscuous. The question wasn't who had Kelly screwed, it was who hadn't she screwed. Even back in high school, he bet everyone knew that.

Okay, he planned to read one more page, and then he would close his eyes for a while. He was not going to think about his cousin or Lizzy. He needed to let everything he'd read sink in. The next page was a list of names, mostly Mac's classmates, Stan, Kyle, Harry, Ford, Grant, Jackson, all crossed through as if his father had considered everyone in his high school to be a suspect and then had one by one systematically crossed them off the list. Yes, his father had questioned him, but his name wasn't listed. It must have floored his father when he admitted he'd taken Kelly parking at Marston's Tunnel. The only problem was, it wasn't everything his father thought. In fact, it wasn't *any*thing like his father probably thought. When he thought it about now, even with only himself for company, the entire episode left him a bit embarrassed.

If Kelly had ever told anyone about his time with her, he would have been the laughing stock and certainly not thought of as the hero of the class or the idol of the football team and super shooter of the basketball team.

The thought stopped him short. And he flipped his own notebook to a page with the headline MOTIVE. Kelly had a mean mouth. She was spoiled with a catty attitude, as confirmed by Lizzy with the 'fucking bore' comment. He hadn't really wanted to be with her, hadn't been turned on by her kiss. It was just that all the other guys on the football team were talking about her and comparing notes. He wanted to be in the loop, too. After he'd gotten alone with her, it seemed all he could think about was getting done and being away from her.

Perhaps there had been a guy who performed even worse than he did, someone she threatened to expose. He could still hear that high-pitched sneer: *wait until I tell all your friends what a loser you are. That you can't even get it up unless I use my mouth...*

She had that power over people. She'd laugh and threaten, then sashay off. She'd run her tongue over her lips and make every guy in class horny with need to get within five feet of her. Mac closed his eyes and thought of that hour with her, parked in the same place where she'd later died. After two kisses, he'd been ready to leave. He'd even started his truck.

Then she'd said, "Wait...Let me show you something..."

And he hadn't been able to leave for another hour. She'd used her mouth to get his plumbing in working order while he sat there with his eyes closed and thought of other girls. That had been only way. He told his father he never would have handed over his class ring to her. After all, he'd only received it two weeks before. Even in his memory, he wasn't certain he would have told her no. It seemed no one ever could.

When he awoke with sunlight in his eyes, he was laying on the notebooks, the list of names smeared with his drool. And a dream of Marston's Tunnel fading away.

Chapter Nine

Tuesday

Neither Lizzy nor Tony was tired. It was a bit early to open, but they decided to put their energy to good use.

She made pumpkin spice coffee. And the tea of the day was called Fall Fruit and Spice, a nice blend of apples and cinnamon. Within a short time, with the two of them working together, the bakery air was filled with the rich aromas of bread, coffee, and spice. Lizzy made her well-known pastry pretzels, pastry in the shape of pretzels sprinkled with cinnamon and sugar or drizzled with white laced icing.

Doing something with her hands—shaping the pretzels—calmed her mind.

"How are you doing?" Tony asked. "Because you've been up all night, and I can handle this if you want to go get some sleep."

Lizzy took a deep breath. "No. I'm not too tired. Besides, I need to be here. I need to keep busy and enjoy a nice cup of tea. Can you stay today? I plan to talk to Stan and tell him we can always be friends, but there won't be anything more."

"Are you worried he's going to take it badly? I mean, am I going to have to defend you or something?"

She chuckled. "I don't...No, I don't think so. Besides, thanks to Kelly Mattis, I think every woman in town has taken some sort of self-defense class, including me. Dad made sure of that, remember?"

"I remember thinking all the dads in town must have gotten together and made it a priority for every girl in our class after that."

"Not that I expect to have to use any of it on Stan, which is I good thing since I'm not sure I remember much of it." She paused and signed. "I really don't know what to expect with him. Like you said, he's always so nice. I admit I really didn't think about it until you said something, but it's like he's almost too polite, which might be why I don't feel any spark for him. It's like everything I say, he just smiles and says, 'Whatever you want, Lizzy.' I have the feeling when I tell him I won't be dating him anymore, he'll just smile and say that same thing."

Tony shrugged. "Maybe. I'm here for you no matter what."

"Thanks," she said, wishing she knew how she actually felt. It was an odd combination of dread and relief. The truth was she should never have agreed to start seeing Stan in the first place. She'd never been interested, and never felt any interest—in anyone.

Then Mac had sauntered into her bakery. And whatever had fallen asleep inside her was awake and hungry. For him.

Damn him.

While Lizzy and Tony served coffee and pie and breakfast to their regulars, Mac sat in an empty office in the Mossy Point Consolidated High School staring at a computer screen. It was times like this he was grateful for technology. Someone had had the foresight to put photos onto computer discs for safekeeping. And while whoever had been in charge of the yearbook ten years ago might have only used a few photos per page, every picture taken, either by the yearbook staff or donated by others throughout his junior and senior years, had been saved and put onto the disc.

At the same time, the trip down memory lane was painful. There were at least fifty photos of the homecoming dance, couples locked in each other's arms and dancing, oblivious to the photographer. He and Lizzy were in over a dozen of them. How young they looked. How innocent. Considering how close to the surface his memory of this night was, it could have been yesterday, not almost eleven years. And why it even bothered him, he didn't know. A lot of water had passed under that bridge, and he hadn't given his high school days a second thought in a very long time. At least not until he'd kissed Lizzy up near Marston's Tunnel.

He shouldn't do this. He closed his eyes for a long moment and took a long, deep breath.

He concentrated on the case. He opened his eyes and forced himself to study everyone else—every*thing* else.

Two hours later, he rubbed his eyes and leaned back in the chair. Then he retrieved his own a flash drive from his pocket and copied every file so he could study each again at his leisure. After all, right then as he waited for his leg to heal, it was one thing he had—time. As for the case so far, he had zilch. At least he knew everyone who was at the dance. So many people he'd forgotten were brought back to him via those still shots—John Hillsworth and Mary Gowen, not together at the dance, but now married, Susan Rugdy had been killed in a car accident the year after graduation, and Tim Tennies married Sylvia Dittleman and now had five kids.

It amazed him how all these memories touched him, all things told to him via his brother or his dad or his mom or via social media or the town newspaper which he could read online. So many details about his hometown and its inhabitants swirled through his brain with his photo study; it was almost like he'd never left. It was certainly like he hadn't been gone for the last decade.

And while he'd learned it wasn't exactly easy going back down this road into the past, to see himself with Lizzy, to see all the friends he'd left behind, he at least discovered her brother, Antonio, had been at the dance. He was in one photo.

Talking to Kelly Mattis and holding her hand.

****

No matter how much Mac wanted to ignore it, or how much he wished it wasn't so, Antonio Signorino remained his only suspect, his only lead. It wasn't much. Hell, it was damn near anorexic. He appeared to be the only guy remotely near Kelly at the dance. Mac wasn't stupid, he knew it didn't come close to being evidence. It wasn't even really a lead. Neither was the idea that Tony attended to Columbia University in Missouri for a year while there was a murder there.

It was a place to start. Maybe he should simply give him a call, invite him out for a beer to pick his brain, see what he thought about Kelly, and what he had to say about his year at Columbia.

Hell, he wished for another direction to take. Not only did this feel *wrong*, it felt like a waste of time. What would Tony's motive be? In the photo, he appeared nothing but friendly toward Kelly. There was nothing out of the ordinary with the way he held her hand. If anything, Kelly looked bored or impatient with *him*. Maybe that was the problem. Perhaps he wanted to dance with her, wanted to be with her, and she brushed him off. It wasn't much of a motive or reason to cut through someone with a knife, but in his career, he'd seen people kill for less reason. He planned to spend the rest of the day following Tony. What could it hurt since he didn't know what else to do? He also didn't have anything else to do.

Following him in the afternoon wasn't hard. He stayed in the bakery.

From his truck parked across the street, the rich aromas of pastries and coffee made Mac's mouth water. When he saw Lizzy through the window smile at a man he recognized as Mr. Jenkins from the hardware store, Mac licked his lips. She'd told him to stay out of her bakery.

He considered going in and getting a coffee, just to show her he could.

The long-gone, rebel teenage boy who would blatantly ignore her instructions to stay out of her bakery was gone. He was over her. But damn it all to hell, the man of now wanted her.

He had to keep reminding himself he was here to watch Tony.

That didn't make it any easier.

At four o'clock, Tony flipped the sign that hung in the door to read CLOSED. A short time later, he exited the front door. Lizzy gave him a quick hug before she locked it behind him.

Tony took off on foot heading south down the main drag.

Mac spent the next twenty minutes maneuvering the streets he knew like the back of his hand, following, catching up, watching, losing, and then finding Tony again after he had to sidetrack around a street that was closed due to a broken water main. When Tony hiked up the walk of a restored two-story house across town from the bakery, Mac parked at the curb and killed the engine.

Mac watched as Tony was greeted just inside the door by a woman Mac remembered from high school. Tiffany Harper.

To Mac's surprise, she greeted Tony with a warm smile and chummy rub down his arm.

Is this where Tiffany lived? Then Mac remembered reading in the weekly online issue of the Mossy Point Tribune, Tiffany had married Dane Kizer about two or three years ago. Mac also remembered seeing Tiffany and Dane dancing together in the Homecoming dance photos earlier. He had never been friends with Dane, but they'd been cordial. Dane played baseball whereas Mac participated in football and basketball. Mac knew he and Tiffany had dated all through the senior year.

If Antonio was visiting Tiff in the afternoon, maybe things weren't working out for Tiffany and Dane after all.

Mac knew he was again jumping to conclusions. Tony worked IT when he wasn't helping out in the bakery. He could very well be fixing the Kizers' home computer, putting in a new router for Wi-Fi—or loading on a new game for Dane to play. Mac remembered Dane was really into the virtual games.

Did all women greet the local computer geek with a smile like that and a welcoming rub down his arm?

Maybe.

Maybe he should give up this crazy idea, enjoy some time with his parents, go have supper with his brother who lived a half hour away, and just share a few beers with some former classmates before he tucked his tail between his legs and headed back to Quantico, let his leg heal somewhere else. He didn't owe Kelly Mattis a thing.

He sucked in a breath and jumped, startled, when a knock on the passenger window returned him to the present in a snap.

He was taken aback even more to see Tony standing there. Hell, he must be losing his touch. It seemed he allowed himself to be too comfortable back in his hometown. He hadn't even noticed Tony had come back outside. Maybe he should give up trying to find out who killed Kelly Mattis. He wouldn't be the first to leave the case unsolved.

Before he could touch the button on the armrest to open the window on the passenger door, Tony opened the door and climbed into the truck to sit with him, slamming the door behind him. There was a long moment of silence as the two of them seemed to measure one another up. Mac slid his hand back and forth along the steering wheel, doing his best not to feel like the cat caught with his paw in the canary cage.

"We didn't get much time to talk last night," Tony said.

"No."

"How long are you in town? Is it really just for the reunion and picnic this weekend, like you said yesterday when you moseyed into the bakery?"

"Yeah. Maybe longer. I don't know."

Tony seemed to absorb his reply. "Right." His hard gaze at Mac never wavered. "Would you care to tell me, then, why you're spending the little time you've got following me around town when you could be catching up with relatives and friends? Because if you wanted to catch up with me, you should have stopped me two blocks back."

"I wasn't—"

"Oh, come on, Mac. Don't bullshit me. Any idiot could have seen you. A few probably did. Is this about Lizzy?"

"No." Another one-word reply. He was getting damned good at them.

"Then what?"

Again, they were quiet for a moment. Somewhere outside a dog barked, muffled through the closed truck window next to Tony. It was a nice fall day. Mac's window was the only one open a few inches.

Then Tony let out an exasperated, "Oh...fuck. You're digging into Kelly Mattis's murder, aren't you? Seeing if you can find anything new. Don't try and deny it. I'm one of the few people you stayed in contact with, remember? I knew you took the FBI test. Then you kind of fell off the grid. After that, whenever I hear from you, it's just vague shit—everything's fine and you're between jobs, blah, blah, blah. We were friends. I hope we still are, but don't treat me like I'm stupid."

"I'm not." Finally, more than one word. Was it progress?

"So, what? I'm a suspect?"

How to reply? This was not how this was supposed to work. Mac was supposed to follow Tony, who would lead him to something incriminating. But damn, Mac felt like the criminal.

"Yes." It was another one-word answer, but was more direct.

It didn't appear to surprise Tony. "Care to tell me why or how, what the hell puts me on your radar?"

Mac didn't beat around the bush. There was no reason to even try. "You took metals class and made jewelry. Then when you were at the University of Missouri, there was another murder, like Kelly's. And you were with her at the homecoming dance."

Tony's dark eyes were endless. "That's all you've got? More than twenty people were in metals class. You were one of them, or have you forgotten? And there were a few hundred students in the freshman class at Mizzou when I was there, three hundred in the Chemistry 101 class alone. I took it with Sara Gibson, the murder victim I think you're referring to."

"I know it's a long shot."

"It's a real long shot in the wrong damned direction. I didn't kill either of them. I haven't killed anyone. And I hate to point it out to you, but you were also at the dance. I'm just wondering, what does metals class have to do with Kelly's murder?"

"She was wearing a bracelet when her body was found."

"She was allergic."

"You knew that?"

Tony shrugged. "Yes. She told me because I did make a bracelet—more than one as a matter of fact—in metals class and offered to give one to her. She took it and thanked me, but told me she could never wear it. She said she'd break out in hives and itch clear into next week if she had it against her skin. Did you know her mom had a special class ring made for her out of porcelain?"

"No. Sounds like the two of you were friends." Mac didn't think Kelly had any true friends.

"I'm probably the only guy in the entire class who didn't have sex with her. I'm probably the only guy who just talked to her." He let out a hard sigh. "I think I'm the only guy she talked to, just talked."

"Why do you suppose that was?" Mac had to ask. "I mean, was it because you found her to be a nice person when so many others didn't?"

He saw Tony bite his bottom lip as he contemplated an answer. "I wasn't interested in her. She knew that. So, I wasn't competition or a conquest."

Mac watched him from across the seat as a car slowly drove past outside. "Oh? Not interested at all? I didn't think there was a guy in the entire school who didn't sniff out Kelly's handouts."

Tony met his gaze evenly. "It seems back then, both Kelly and I were interested in the same guy. You."

To say he was shocked would have been the understatement of the year, but Mac managed to keep it tucked inside him with a deep breath and a clench of his jaw.

"The only difference was," Tony continued calmly, "she really expected you to ask her to the dance. So, when you didn't and you showed up with my sister, she was...enraged would have been putting it mildly. I watched her at the dance because I was concerned about my sister. I figured Kelly might do something, being the malicious bitch everyone knew her to be. Honestly, I was surprised she didn't toss a drink on Lizzy or try to scratch her eyes out. As for me, I never expected anything at all from you. I knew that being a friend was as close as I was ever going to get. And I accepted that."

Mac worked to digest Tony's bombshell. It wasn't easy. Trying to stay on topic, he asked, "Who'd she leave with?"

"I have no idea. One minute she was there with me. And I was trying to convince her to dance with me, trying to take her mind off killing my sister. While I was busy watching you with Lizzy, she left. And if you don't believe me, you can ask Dane Kizer. I hung with him until I headed home, which was about a quarter of midnight. It wasn't until after one when my dad and Lizzy got home that I learned Kelly was dead. And if you're going to ask me if she seemed pre-occupied, the answer is yes, she did. She always did. After all, she was always worried there might be a girl who was prettier than she was, and she was just as worried there might be one guy who didn't notice her."

"That's true," Mac had to agree. "What else did she talk about?"

Tony shrugged. "Just stuff. She said she planned to leave town."

"Leave town. When? How?"

"I have no idea. I thought it was just talk, like everyone else's talk about how we all planned to escape as soon as our tassels were switched to the other side."

"And, if she did have a plan, how would she pay for that?"

"I don't know that, either. Maybe she figured out she could sell it instead of always giving it away. She didn't tell me." He paused. "I'm not your killer, but I'd sure like to help you find him or her. I'm tired of that unsolved mystery hanging over this town like a dark cloud."

Mac wouldn't normally believe someone who just said he wasn't the killer. After all, killers confessed sometimes, but not that easily. And they almost always denied it. However, he believed Tony, especially given the evidence against him wouldn't hold water. Just to be on the safe side, he did plan to talk to Dane Kizer.

"Speaking of Dane Kizer, I thought you guys were friends, especially if you hung out after the dance. And now you're what? Banging his wife in the afternoon?" Mac wasn't certain why he asked. He just needed to know how things stood before he asked Dane about being with Tony on dance night.

Tony grinned. "Yes, but it's not what you think."

"Oh, what do I think?"

"You think we're cheating behind his back."

"Aren't you?"

Tony was quiet for a long moment as he stared out the window before him. "Hell," he said finally, "I haven't lied to you. Ever. I'm not going to start now. The truth is Dane and Tiffany and I have been lovers for years."

It was another shock Mac had to tuck down under his belt and work to keep from showing on his face.

"Dane and Tiff got married instead of me and Tiff because his parents accepted our threesome better. If I had married Tiffany, my parents would have expected...I don't know, something more traditional. If I had married Dane, my father would have disowned me. This way, I maintain my apartment, which makes me the perfect bachelor too busy to get married. I spend a lot of time over here with them. I even have my own room. I'll be honest, I'd love to skip down the street with both of us holding Tiff's hands. I don't think the town is ready for that. Even though the two of them say they don't care what anyone else thinks, I have two businesses in this town, and my sister owns half of one. I won't chance that." He paused and took a deep breath. When he spoke again, his words were filled with tight emotion. "And I'd love to take them both to Florida and spend Christmas with my parents, but I don't think my parents are any readier for that than the town is. So, right now, just like long ago when my friendship with you was enough, this has to be enough. And, if you want to go out and blab it around and let my secret out, go ahead. I won't try and stop you. But I sure hope you don't."

Mac had to remember to breathe. "Your secret's safe with me. Does Lizzy know?"

"We've never talked about it, but she knows me better than anyone. She always refers to Dane and Tiff as my *friends* and for the past several years, she bought Christmas presents for them."

Again, they sat as quiet seconds ticked by, and Mac digested all this new information. This was certainly a small-town secret that sent him for a loop even though it didn't send him in any new direction to help him solve his cold case. Hell, he'd had no idea Tony had an attraction to him. Had Tony even been perhaps jealous of his own sister because Mac had asked her to the dance? Perhaps that was a question better left unanswered. Still, Tony had done a damned fine job of hiding his feelings.

"Anything else you want to know, Mac?"

Not trusting his voice just then, he only shook his head. Then something did come to him. "You know IT. Do you know how to find people?"

"I managed to stay in touch with you, didn't I?" Tony grinned.

"I know everyone says Stan's dad ran off, probably to Florida, probably found a new girlfriend. I know everyone, especially Stan's mom, was happy to see him gone. He left that fall after Kelly's murder. If you really want to help me, see if you can track him down. I don't know if it will help with the case or not. George Hattersfield and Marvin Wellsburg, as well as Stan's dad, left within a year of the murder for reasons unknown. I want to be able to cross them off the list."

"I'll see what I can find out. Later. You can even give me your whole list of names if you want. As for now, would you like to come inside for supper? Tiff's made a big pan of lasagna and garlic bread that will melt in your mouth."

Mac thought about it, then returned Tony's grin. "Lasagna sounds great. Thanks." He started to climb out of the truck, but Tony's hand on his arm stopped him.

"The town may not be able to handle my lifestyle or the fact I can and do love two people, but I don't let it stop me from loving them or from being with them. I work around it. If Kelly's murder taught me anything, it was that I don't want to waste a single moment. You shouldn't either. I think you and my sister have wasted enough time. I know I'm certainly tired of watching her wandering around, searching for someone who remotely makes her feel the way she felt about you."

"She's with Stan." Each word felt like a knife slicing open his gut and leaving him cold.

"I doubt she's ever *been with* Stan. And, as of today, not at all. When I left, that's where she was heading after she cleaned up a few things in the kitchen, to his shop to break things off with him. She said even if things didn't work out with you, she could never live a lie with him. So quit wasting time." He let go of Mac's arm, opened the door, and slid out of the truck.

Mac climbed out, too. He smelled the rich, wonderful aroma of lasagna the moment Tiffany opened the door for them. And she greeted Mac with a hug

Chapter Ten

Lizzy rolled her shoulders. After preparing the dough for tomorrow's pastries and crusts, getting the bakery in order, checking inventory, making an order list, and cleaning the kitchen, she was ready for a light supper with her feet up. She had the ingredients ready for tomorrow's Caesar chicken wraps. They weren't the usual bakery offerings but people who stopped in for coffee or tea didn't always want a donut or a cruller. She could fix herself a chicken wrap. That'd be easy and light. Then maybe a bubble bath.

Only then would she allow herself to think about Mac. She had to make a decision—trust him again or forget him.

She already discovered she couldn't forget him.

First, she needed to do the thing that had plagued her all day. She had to let Stan off the hook. It wasn't that she'd put it off all day. She simply needed to wait until everything else was finished so she could make it a priority. And he hadn't forced her hand by coming into the coffee shop as he usually did.

Now she had no excuse. She had the feeling perhaps he knew it was coming; he hadn't texted or called her all day. Truth be told, she hadn't noticed he'd never sent his usual HI text, complete with smiley face, until now when she checked her phone.

She didn't want to text him to let him know she was coming. She just set out walking, soaking up the fall sunshine, and allowing the fresh air to clear her mind as she made her way the two blocks up Main Street to his shop. Halfway there, she met his brother.

"Hi, Elliot." Somehow, she was a little relieved to meet him here and not at the shop. She didn't want him to hear the conversation. It was bad enough this conversation had to happen at all. She didn't need an audience. And Elliot would probably have his own input, which she also didn't need because she had the feeling he liked her and Stan together. He wouldn't understand her reasons for the break up.

"Lizzy! Hi!"

"Is Stan still at the shop?"

"Yeah. He said he was going to feed all the cats before he locked up. He sent me home to help Mom with supper. He knows taco night is my favorite."

"Sounds yummy."

"You could come eat with us if you want. We always have enough for lots of tacos."

"Maybe some other time." *Probably never after I tell Stan we're only going to be friends.* She tried to smile. "But thanks."

"Okay. See you later."

"See you." Lizzy watched him lumber off, happily heading home for his favorite meal. A moment later, she stepped onto the pavement in front of Stan's body shop. The big sign out front said Gresden's Body Work and Detailing.

The two overhead garage doors were up.

The smell of paint, something like burning metal, and other indefinable chemicals touched her before she stepped into the shade inside them. "Stan?"

No answer.

It took a moment for her eyes to adjust to the dim after being out in the late afternoon sunlight. She blinked and looked around. In the far corner, four cats sat eating from dishes filled with what was obviously cat food. "Stan?"

Still no answer.

She didn't come here often, but she'd been inside the building a few times, enough to know where the office was. She headed there now, the lingering chemical smells burning her nose, her sneakers barely making a sound on the concrete floor. She carefully watched where she stepped. She knew Elliot did his best to sweep and clean. She also knew anything dropped on the floor—metal shavings, paint thinner, whatever, would be slippery.

The door to the office was ahead of her in the corner of the building across from the work area. The top half of the door was beveled glass, rippled in such a way, it would let in light. She, however, could not see into the office beyond the black letters that stated OFFICE.

"Stan?" She knocked lightly before she grasped the knob, turned it and entered.

Seeing him seated beside his desk with a cat in his hand was surprising enough. While he was thought of as the crazy cat man, at least by Elliot, she hadn't really ever seen him as a 'cat person' at all. And seeing him sitting there with a yellow striped cat in one hand, his fingers around the cat's neck stopped her in her tracks.

He was choking the cat. Squeezing...squeezing...ignoring the way the cat was clawing at his hand, his wrist, his arm and equally ignoring the blood on him from the scratches.

His fly was open. And with his free hand, he stroked himself as he choked the cat.

His eyes were closed. His groans filled the small space. In fact, he was so lost in his actions, he didn't even know she'd stepped into his office, didn't know she was there.

Until she let out a gasp.

His eyes flew open.

He stared at her for a long moment as if he didn't recognize her. He didn't even appear to know where he was. And he certainly wasn't like the soft-spoken Stan she knew, the one who always offered her a smile and folded his napkin when he finished his coffee. His face was red. His eyes and the veins of his neck bulged. He gritted his teeth and, in his grimace, she saw almost all of them. He was like a hideous Halloween monster showing his teeth. In his hand, the cat still struggled like mad, scratching the hell out his arm, and letting out little huffing sounds as Stan squeezed its vocal cords. Blood from the scratches on his hand dripped to his desk. Lizzy took this all in in a matter of perhaps two heartbeats.

Then Stan hurled the cat away.

The action and the sound of the poor animal colliding with the wall shook her out of whatever shock held her in place. Lizzy raced toward the door. She got in two steps and managed to get her hand around the door knob of the office door before he grabbed her and swung her around to face him. He shoved her back against the wall near the door. In her thoughts, she registered the window with the word OFFICE on it as it shattered behind her.

The slam knocked the wind from her lungs and left her gasping for a breath. Not that she was given much time to think about taking one. She wasn't given much time to think at all before his hands were on *her* throat.

Time seemed to slow. Perhaps it even stopped. She didn't know. Maybe the world stopped revolving around the sun. In the one breath she managed before his hands cut off her air, the copper scent of the blood on his hand burned her nose. Her chest felt as if it was on fire, too. His hands were slick and hot on the flesh of her throat. His breath was equally as warm on her face. The acid scent of it caused her stomach to roil.

She saw his eyes, the rage on his face. He wanted to kill her. In that slow-motion instant of clarity, she saw his fly was still open. His erection...Oh, God.

"I saw you with him out by Marston's Tunnel, you fucking slut. What were you doing, reliving old times out there? You've never kissed me like that. Never."

Black spots danced before her eyes. Then instinct took hold, linked with the need to breathe. And while it may have been years since she'd gone to her self-defense class, it may as well have been yesterday. Later, she would be surprised at just how efficiently and quickly it rushed back to her. It was as if she heard the voice of Jace Wittemeyer, the instructor inside her head. *Tuck the chin. Make hooks with both hands. Pluck the attackers hands away in a snappy motion. Do it now! Don't hesitate! End the threat! Then make sure he can't attack you again!*

Her actions took him by surprise. He was still crazed, leaving her to wonder if he'd taken something or smoked something, his breaths coming in puffs that sounded a lot like those of the cat he'd held, only louder. Other instructions from her self-defense class poured through her thoughts like a swift river. Target areas...She popped him in the nose with the palm of her hand. Less than a second later, she hit him in the throat, just as she'd been taught.

He gasped, and still held her, but his grip loosened. She sent her palm upward under his chin, snapping his head back, and beneath his huffing breaths, she heard his teeth snap together with a loud click. It was enough to send him a few steps backwards. She saw again his fly was still open. Her kick landed squarely there, on what was obviously a lonely boy covered with petroleum jelly.

He sucked in air, sounding like he'd just broke the surface of the water after being at the bottom of the ocean.

Before he could even begin to recover, she delivered another kick with the heel of her foot to his left knee, the wounded one, the one that made him lose his scholarship. It sent him to the floor, but he didn't seem to notice as he stared up at her, his hands cupping himself.

Lizzy tried to run, only to discover that she couldn't quite get the message to her brain. She slid down the wall and stared at the man before her in disbelief. The breath she forced in was heavy and loud. It seemed to be what she needed so she took another. Then she clumsily scrambled to her feet and ran.

Chapter Eleven

Mac headed home after enjoying supper with Tiffany, Antonio, and Dane. The lasagna had been everything Tony promised it would be and the garlic bread really did melt in his mouth. The company, the memories they shared, and the wine had been like icing on a fun birthday cake. It left him questioning what he was really doing here. This was home. This was what was important—friends, conversation, good times. Perhaps it might be best if he left the dead buried in the cemetery and simply concentrated on the here and now and living. The only thing missing from the dinner he'd just enjoyed had been Lizzy sitting next to him. And it wasn't as if he had any new clues in the cold case of Kelly Mattis.

He wondered how Lizzy's break up with Stan had gone. He wondered if he had a chance. He wondered if it was even wise of him to consider it.

Mac slammed on the brakes to avoid hitting a woman who suddenly barreled out from between two parked cars. The rear wheels of his truck didn't stop at the same time the front ones did. The back of his truck fishtailed to the right. The last time he'd felt so out of control while driving, there had been seven inches of snow and ice covering the highway. His heart seemed to lurch in his chest.

Then he recognized her. He was going to run over Lizzy! Somehow, he managed to get control of the truck and stopped.

Lizzy, however, didn't. She ran into the hood, bounced back, and landed on that perfect ass of hers in the grass just off the curb.

In the next second, he was out of the truck and at her side.

Her expression was a mixture of terror and disbelief, her eyes wild. And before he could stop her, hell, before he could reach her, she scrambled to her feet and tried to run.

He caught her by the arm. "Lizzy!"

She screamed, swung her free hand, and cuffed him on the side of the face, sending his thoughts and his world spinning. It took a good two or three seconds to regain control. At least he managed to keep a hold on her. All the while she screamed, "No! No!"

At the same time, he yelled her name. When she swung at him again, he caught her wrist, then her other, hugging her back against the front of him with her arms crossed in front of her in a smooth defensive hold. He moved in a knick of time when she tried to stomp on his foot. "Lizzy. It's me. It's Mac. Listen to my voice. It's me. I won't hurt you." His words got through.

"Mac?"

"Yes."

She sagged against him. Her breaths were still loud and heaving. She trembled in his arms. His face smarted like a son of a bitch.

Beyond Lizzy, he saw that the woman who lived in the white house across the street stood on her porch, obviously drawn to the sounds of his squealing tires and the yelling. He recognized her. "Mrs. Cooper, call 9-1-1," he yelled.

She hurried into the house again.

"Lizzy, what the hell happened?"

"Stan...Stan..."

He let go of her wrists, but noticed immediately she wobbled as if she couldn't stand. He turned her to face him and held her on her feet by holding her arms. He took in her face, the blood and red fingerprints on her throat. "Stan did this to you? Blood?" Instant rage burned through him like a volcano erupting. He'd kill that bastard...

"It's his blood," she let out.

"It's obvious he choked you."

"Yes, I...I got out of his hold. I hit him and kicked him."

"Because you broke up with him?" Unbelievable...

"I didn't even get that far."

She doubled over, breathing loudly, covering her face with both hands. The stance revealed more of her neck. He saw the beginnings of bruises and had to suck in a breath. If he didn't understand she needed him, he'd head over to Stan's shop and make a few bruises of his own.

"I went to tell him I wasn't going out with him anymore, but I caught him jacking off in the office."

"What?"

"While he strangled a cat. Then he tried to strangle me. I thought he was going to kill me. He saw us. Up by the tunnel, kissing. He was so filled with rage. I've never seen him like that."

Mac fought the urge to go see it for himself and give a bit of it back to Stan. However, he remained where he was.

For at that moment, Officer Jake Swornson rushed up and skidded to a stop in his police cruiser, lights and siren blaring.

****

It was after midnight when Tony noticed he had a new voice mail from Lizzy and listened to it. Within minutes, he dressed, kissed his lovers good-bye, jogged to his nearby apartment to his car, and sped to Mac's small loft apartment over the barn at the orchard.

Mac was waiting. He opened the door and placed his index finger against his lips in the universal sign to stay quiet. Then Mac stepped aside to reveal Lizzy tucked into the bed in the far corner, sleeping soundly. With another hand motion, Mac indicated he should follow.

Pausing to grab two bottles of beer from a small fridge, Mac led him through the small apartment to the tiny balcony on the far end where two lawn chairs sat. Tony wondered if the structure would hold them both because of the creaking sound when they stepped out, but Mac didn't seem to be worried.

The night was bright with the September moon. Clouds filled the western sky; for now, stars twinkled above. The air was fresh and smelled of apples and whatever animals Mac's dad housed below in the orchard in a petting zoo for the little kids. A soft breeze caused the trees to dance in the moonlight. Mac handed a beer to Tony and closed the sliding door behind them. Tony didn't speak until they were both seated.

"Is she all right?" He didn't open the beer, wasn't sure he could keep it in his stomach if he drank it. "She said on her voice mail she'd had to fight Stan and that he choked her. Are you fucking kidding me?"

Mac told him an unbelievable story, even told him how Lizzy had run into the hood of his truck, how she'd cuffed him in his face.

The chuckle Tony let out was bitter and left a sour taste in his mouth. He still didn't open the beer.

Mac did, and took a huge swig.

"I guess those defense classes she took years ago paid off," Tony remarked.

Tony couldn't help but notice the way Mac stared out at the orchard as Mac replied. "I'm certainly glad they did."

"Where's Stan now?" Tony asked.

Mac shrugged. "No one seems to know. He wasn't in the shop by the time Daniels and Swornson got there. Because they don't know I'm FBI, I'm not privy to their information. But I've got a radio and a scanner and can listen in. I don't think they've found him."

"Why aren't you there, trying to find something out? You could just act like a concerned citizen. After all, you could argue you feel as if you're in danger." Tony asked, thinking he might have to do the same thing.

"When Jake Swornson insinuated that Lizzy made more to it than what it was, more or less called it a 'domestic spat,' then made a comment about if women would just do their wifely duty, men wouldn't have these problems, I bit my tongue and left. I know if I hadn't, I'd be out of a job and in a cell, and Jake would have no teeth. And Lizzy would be alone. I also knew Daniels might not think Stan is much of a threat."

"Daniels is such a dick."

"And then there's Swornson..."

"What about him?"

To Tony's amazement Mac revealed another story that had just taken place the previous night involving his young cousin, the cutie who worked at the burger joint. It left his blood boiling. He finally popped open the beer and took a long drink, allowing the cold liquid to attempt to put out the fire. "I had no idea."

Mac finished with, "So warn Tiffany."

Tony shook his head. "What the hell has happened to this town since your dad retired?"

"So far, nothing good. It's like a cloud is hanging over it."

"There's been a cloud hanging over it for eleven years."

They were quiet for a moment, listening to crickets and two distant owls calling to one another. "But my sister's all right."

"Yes. I took her to the clinic. They checked her over really well. She's got some bruises...on her neck. They offered her a sedative, but she refused. She didn't seem to need it anyway. After we finished at the clinic, she insisted we go back and find the cat he'd been strangling. We took it to the vet and now the orchard has a new yellow cat. Unless she takes it home with her. She didn't argue with me when I said she was coming home with me, although she made me stop by her place so she could get a change of clothes. She crashed right after a hot shower and a hot cup of tea. She's been sleeping ever since. I don't think she's even shifted position." He met Tony's gaze. "Not that I want her close to Stan again, but from the sounds of it, she whipped the crap out of him."

"Good. What's next?"

"Aside from letting her finish him off, I don't know. I do know she's not leaving my sight."

"Good," Tony said again. The only available light was that which filtered out through the sliding glass door behind them. Tony met

Mac's gaze through the shadows. "What about the end of the week or next week when you leave and disappear again, going back under whatever rock you've been hiding under all these years?"

Mac stayed silent for a long moment. "That's a good question. Maybe I'll take her with me."

Tony wasn't so sure Lizzy would leave the bakery or him, her twin. Even for Mac. Either way, his leaving should prove to be interesting.

Then Mac added, speaking so softly, Tony was certain it was an afterthought that was beginning to glow in his thoughts. "Or maybe I won't go at all."

He grinned but didn't know if Mac could see it. "You certainly know how to liven up a place, don't you?"

"If I had known my return would cause so much excitement, I'd have come back years ago."

"Tell her to stay here tomorrow and rest. I'll handle the bakery. If I know her—which I do—all I'll have to do anyway is serve the customers. She's got everything else ready to go."

"Thanks. I'll convince her she needs to stay and help my dad, who has a few busloads of school kids coming tomorrow to pick apples."

"She'll probably want to come to the bakery just to get them all donuts," Tony said it lightheartedly, but in a sense, it was probably true.

After the first raindrops began to plop onto the balcony, Tony and Mac headed inside. At the door, Tony paused and gazed across the room at his sister. The yellow cat she'd saved slept curled up at the foot of the bed.

Yes, he loved Tiffany and Dane. Yes, he adored his parents and cared about the town, however, Lizzy had shared the womb with him. She held his heart as no one else ever could. He considered going over to her, giving her a light kiss, but he held back. The last thing he needed to do after what was obviously a traumatizing ordeal was startle her awake.

"Don't let anything happen to her."

"I won't." Then Mac seemed to catch himself. "*We* won't."

"That's right. We won't."

Then he headed home to be held through the night by Tiff and Dane. For once, he didn't care if anyone noticed his car at their house all night. For once, he didn't care what anyone else thought. Life was too short, too precious, not to spend it beside those you loved.

****

Mac watched Tony leave by way of the loft stairs before he locked the door.

Without a sound, he hesitantly stepped to the side of his bed. Without taking his gaze from Lizzy's sleeping form, he slid his holstered gun off and locked it into the drawer of the nightstand. Her breathing was soft and rhythmic. He could have stood there all night just watching her.

It amazed him how easily she stepped back into his life. He didn't, however, want her like this, not afraid and bruised. He should be a gentleman and sleep in the only other cushioned chair. The last thing he felt was gentlemanly. After he kicked off his shoes and he climbed onto the bed behind her, he did stay on top of the covers while she was tucked beneath them.

In her sleep, she snuggled up against him. A heartbeat later, her hand was out from beneath the quilt, and she latched on to his arm that he draped over her. And she felt pretty perfect tucked up against him, despite the layers of covers between them.

"Mac?" she mumbled.

"I'm here."

The flowery scent of her hair was something he wanted to bury his face in. A deep breath helped him relax. He had to keep reassuring himself she was all right. The loft door was locked. Outside, Ozzie guarded the entire orchard. Stan—or anyone else—couldn't get in, much less up the stairs, without his knowing.

"Don't leave me."

He wasn't even sure she was awake enough to know she spoke to him. He replied to her anyway. "I'm right here."

"Please hold me," she mumbled. "Don't let me go. And don't ever leave me." Then she was back to nothing more than that cadenced breathing.

He was certain he would never sleep, not with Lizzy in his arms, not after what she'd just said. Not after her horrific experience and knowing the cause of it was running around loose somewhere in the dark of night. Spooned against her, her warmth seeming to seep into him and calm him everywhere, the sounds of rain that pattered on the roof above him lulled him to sleep.

Chapter Twelve

Hidden in the shadows, Chief Franklin Daniels stood just inside the woods north of Marston's Tunnel. Clouds masked the moon. The only sounds around him were the rustle of fall leaves in the cool breeze and the whisper of an occasional scampering critter. The rich scent of approaching rain hung in the air. Through the darkness, he stared into the tunnel. He was certain he would be old and gray, forgetful with dementia when he was ninety, and still remember that fateful night Kelly Mattis died. Even now, the memory of all the flashing lights of the police cars left him in a cold sweat.

Sometimes weeks passed without a reminder.

Sometimes, he couldn't get through an hour without needing to grasp something solid to keep from shaking with the memory he couldn't suppress. Things hadn't happened as he thought they would that night. And he'd spent the past decade trying to do right to make up for his mistakes. There wasn't a moment that past by that he didn't wish he could go back and change one night. It wasn't possible, so he made do the best he knew how. He hadn't even known Kelly had been found until later.

Now this thing with Lizzy Signorino happened. He wished he could make it less than what it was, but she was a business owner in town. Everyone knew her. He was pretty certain everyone would see hand prints on her throat. That was not a petty thing he could sweep under the rug with a smile or a wag of his finger.

Standing here in the dark, he was again reminded, just as he'd discovered that night eleven years ago, and many times since, there were no sure promises in life.

It didn't heal to come here. It didn't help him think or clear his mind. It didn't make his days easier. It didn't end his nightmares.

His phone chirped, indicating he had a personal text. He slid his phone from his pocket. The light on the display which revealed the message also lit up the night. Anyone who might have been close would have seen his face.

No one was nearby.

I need your help.

He sucked in a breath. He should ignore the plea or refuse. He also knew it was impossible because his dick hardened with just the thought of the woman who sent the text.

Perhaps it would be best if he took out the gun he carried and swallowed a bullet. It would be the quickest solution.

In the end, he didn't have the courage. At least not right now. As he headed back into town, his footsteps crunching in the foliage, the first raindrops fell with enough force to sting his face.

Chapter Thirteen

Wednesday

Lizzy woke to the sound of a loud *meow,* and the rich aroma of coffee. Her stomach grumbled. Her first thought was that she'd fallen asleep in the bakery, and the coffee was brewing on her timer-set makers.

Then she focused on the wall before her. It was the white-washed planks of Mac's barn-loft apartment. And memories of the previous day slithered through her like a snake. She tried to maintain control of those horrid thoughts.

She'd escaped. She was safe. She was fine. She was with Mac.

Slowly, she rolled over, ignoring the ache and stiffness in her shoulder that hadn't been there before her fighting match with Stan. Golden morning sunlight poured in through the windows on each end of the large, open loft room. She snuggled deeper under the covers—covers that smelled clean and woodsy like Mac.

Then she saw him.

He opened the door and let the cat go out before he lightly stepped back to the corner area designated as a kitchen, complete with counters and a stove, and a vintage mint green colored fridge. A small table with two chairs was set before it. He was barefoot and shirtless, wearing only a pair of jeans. Sweet heavens, he was sexy as hell. His hair was damp, obviously from a recent shower. Rays of morning light streaked over his tanned shoulders, the muscles of his arms, his strong back. He maneuvered a spatula expertly as he flipped a pancake. The yeasty scent of pancakes mixed with the coffee.

Had it been a dream? Had those arms held her in the night? Had he whispered he was there for her?

Those words, that touch, the safety of that embrace had been real. The memory of them sent her heart skipping.

She leaned up and grasped her phone which rested on the nearby nightstand.

Noting the time, she jumped to the edge of the bed. "Oh, my God! I've got to get to the bakery." Her throat felt like her vocal cords were rubbed with sandpaper with each word.

"Not this morning," Mac replied calmly as he tossed her a quick glance over his shoulder. Then he faced the stove again and flipped a pancake. "Tony's got it."

She swallowed hard. The action wasn't heart-stopping painful, but it didn't feel good. "But..." A cool drink sounded like the best remedy.

"No buts," he interrupted. "You're spending the day with me. Here. The rain stopped a few hours ago, which is good since a bunch of school kids are coming to pick apples, but it's supposed to be back later this afternoon. You can take a break from work, allow yourself to get over what happened yesterday, and enjoy some fresh air in the orchard. Take my word for it, it's very therapeutic."

The floor beneath her bare feet was cold. "Who do you think you are, telling me what to do?" She grabbed an empty glass from the table and filled it with water from the nearby tap. The cool liquid helped put out the fire in her throat.

"Aside from the man who almost ran over you yesterday?" He let out a bitter chuckle. "Which I'm doubly glad I didn't, considering I don't know how in the hell I would have explained that one to your father."

She didn't need that reminder, either. It was just that she didn't need someone—anyone—to control her. She was still licking the wounds created when she learned about his letters and that her parents and brother had controlled that part of her life by keeping them from her. She told herself it would never happen again. Too many things had been taken or kept from her. She was done with that. From now on...

"And now that I think about it, I'm also the man who stayed with you last night." He glanced at her over his shoulder. His gaze, although icy blue, held enough heat to melt her into planks beneath her feet.

While she didn't want to be reminded of Stan with his hands on her throat yesterday, or Mac's letters she recently discovered, holding onto the memory of his arms around her through the night was like a warm blanket on cold evening. "You didn't try anything. Don't you want me? Aren't you interested?" she said with a grin, trying to lighten the moment.

He didn't grin back. "That would have been an unfair advantage. I would have been making a victim out of you—twice. The last thing I want to be is in the same category with Stan."

"Tell me he's in jail."

He flipped a pancake. He gave her a slight shrug. "Not that I've heard. Then, I'm not keeping tabs on him this morning."

Somehow, she doubted that. Yesterday after he put together the puzzle she laid out in bits and pieces about what had happened in the office of Stan's shop, she was certain he wanted to go inflict some pain on Stan. Mac wasn't the kind of guy to sit idly by, waiting. He was the quarterback; going for the ball on every play. She stepped closer to him, ignoring the cool air on her legs. She vaguely remembered taking a shower and putting on a shirt he handed to her because she'd been too frazzled to remember one when she grabbed a change of clothes at her place after coming back from the clinic.

"What do you think I should do about him?"

He met her gaze for a long moment before his attention and obviously his nose was reminded of the cooking pancake before him. "What do you mean, what you should do about him?"

"Do you think I should press charges?"

"You have to ask that question? Of course, I guess if you don't want to, I could take it upon myself to simply beat the shit out of him. Or let you."

"I own a business in town; so does he. And he's on the town board. Something like my pressing charges against him could cause divisions. I don't want to do that."

"Something like him really hurting you or someone else could cause problems, too," he reminded her.

"It's not that I don't want to charge him. He deserves to be in jail. He should be in jail. But I need to think about my business, too. And I just wish I could keep this all quiet."

"You can probably try all you want, but you know how news spreads like wild fire through a town like this. And you can spend the morning thinking about how you want to handle things. Give yourself some time to heal."

"All right, I'll spend the day here at the orchard. Just for the record though, you could never be in the same category as Stan." She paused and took another long drink of water. "What if..."

"What if what?"

"What if I want you to touch me?" The question popped out before she could stop it, before she could think. And she wasn't grinning as she spoke the words. "Are you interested? Because I need to know where I stand."

Without taking his gaze from her, he slid the skillet filled with pancakes to a cold burner. She thought perhaps he might just grab her and set her on the table like a piece of nice China, make her his breakfast.

He did turn to her and take her in his arms.

Lizzy could never get over how safe it was to be close to him, how secure she felt tucked in his embrace. While it was true, Stan's actions of the day before left her hesitant and maybe even a little jumpy. Everything about Mac—getting lost in his gaze, taking in the clean man smell of him, feeling the warmth of his touch, all left her feeling grounded and in control. She was no longer a teenage girl, easily swayed by good looks or a kiss or a little flirtation. What happened yesterday with Stan was a horrid thing, but it could have been so much worse. Hell, she might never have known Stan's true nature until after she married him.

She would never have married him. Even if Mac had never come to town, something in her soul told her Stan wasn't what she wanted or needed, which was why their relationship never skipped to the next rock in the bubbling brook of the dating game.

"I am interested. But not today."

She had to clear her throat before she could speak. "Why not today?" Then she slipped out of his embrace just enough to take another drink to sooth her throat. At least it didn't feel like it was on fire any longer. She put the glass back on the nearby table.

"Not in the aftermath of Stan's violence. Right now, I want to keep you safe. I want the episode to be a little further behind you. Because when I touch you—and I *do* plan to touch you—I want you to only think of my touch. When I kiss your throat, I don't want you to be reminded of any pain he gave you there. I want you to only enjoy it."

He cupped her face with one hand. His touch was...breathtaking. She leaned into it.

"I want every part of you feeling every part of me. Nothing else."

Sweet heavens, the man should write poetry, she thought.

Then he kissed her. Warm. Full. Perfect. Wonderful.

The rest of the world stopped.

His kiss was exquisite. This wasn't just a quick, urgent, punishing rush of lips like the one he'd pretty much forced on her when they'd been out by Marston's Tunnel that first evening he got into town. It was exploring, and it stole the breath from her lungs.

It made her feel new, whole somehow. It seemed to touch her in her soul with warm fingers and heal the part that Stan had tried to choke out of her.

When it ended, he held her gaze for a long time. Then he smiled a small smile.

"What?" she asked.

"Kissing you just took me back to..."

"To what?"

"A few weeks ago, I thought there was an open door when it came to you. The only thing is, your kiss took me right through that door and a step forward."

There was something more he wasn't telling her, something specific that triggered the memory of her kissing him, but before she could ask about it, he continued, "I'm not in limbo land anymore. And I know I want to keep moving forward. I do want you, Lizzy, but you've had a traumatic experience."

She chuckled bitterly. "I've had more than one since you waltzed back into town—not that any of them are your fault. In fact, I'm sure I would have discovered all of these things at one time or another. I would have found your letters in the storage unit while I was searching for an attachment for my pastry mixer. I have no doubt I would have eventually noticed all the scratches on Stan's arms." She let out a loud sigh. "I certainly hope I would have learned about his need to jack off the way he does. If I had stayed with him long enough, which I doubt. There simply was never any spark between us."

He crossed his arms over his chest and faced her squarely. "I'm just saying before we take another step, you need a little time. The last thing I want between us is any regret. Especially when you might need to deal with emotions regarding the violent—"

"You're damn right it was violent. My throat still hurts. And I admit it's left me badly shaken, but I can't let it control the rest of my life." She paused and scratched her neck.

"Thanks to you and knowing that cat is safe, the fear is already beginning to fade. The bruises will, too. Please don't treat me like a child who doesn't know what's best for her. I know my own feelings. Do you know what I find worse than having Stan choke me, choke a cat? I don't care if he needs to jack off all day. God, I still hear the sound of that poor animal hitting the wall..."

"What? What's worse?"

"Knowing him almost my whole life, and never having a clue as to that—that's worse. Do you know what else?" She stared at him, taking in his bare chest. She grabbed her glass of water and took another cool drink.

"Tell me."

"In that moment when I knew I had to do something or I might die, I thought about..."

"About what?"

She took an easy breath. It felt good to talk, good to let it all out. "He saw us out at Marston's Tunnel. He saw us kiss. He yelled at me that I never kissed him like that—which is true. When his hand was on my throat and he was staring at me with such a crazed expression, the thought that I wanted more kisses like that. I wanted just plain more of that feeling. And I wanted it with you."

The room was quiet for two heartbeats, and damn him, he didn't say anything. So, she went on, "What was worse was the idea I might never feel that again. Yes, he scared the hell out of me. I have no doubt, I'll have a few nightmares in my future, but I didn't have one last night because you held me all night. You make me feel human. And safe. You make me feel alive. I felt it the moment you stepped into my shop. That, Mac, is what I want. If there is one thing Stan showed me it's that I don't want to waste another moment not having what I want because it can all be gone in an instant." She set the glass down again, this time with a heavy thud.

She stepped closer to him. Her breasts touched his chest. There was the thin cotton of the shirt he'd given her last night to wear between his skin and hers, but damn if she couldn't feel his warmth. She leaned against him, leaned the side of her face to his hard, perfect chest and listened to his heart beating as she breathed in the enticing scent of him and soap. "Let's please quit wasting time."

Mac held her closer, putting his arms around her as he closed his eyes and breathed in a deep breath which filled him with the alluring scent of something musky. She was all soft woman. And when she took in a breath, her nipples...

He tried to breathe. He was trying to protect her. He was trying to stay the cop on duty. Until Stan was found, he planned to protect her. He needed to protect her if the police—Jake Swornson, who obviously thought women were toys to be played with—considered this nothing more than a lover's spat. All he had to do was see the handprints on her throat to know it was more than that. In order to do his job, he needed to keep the head on his shoulders thinking straight. He couldn't let the one in his jeans confuse things.

"I have to protect you, Lizzy."

"Damn straight, you do," she agreed. "However, I do know a bit about how to protect myself, too; and I'll do it again if necessary."

"You don't make this easy." He breathed in the flowery scent of her hair and wanted to lose himself in it, in her.

"Oh?"

"I'm thinking you should give up the bakery and become a lawyer."

She softly laughed in his arms, and he felt more of her breasts—all of her, really—against him, like a piece of a puzzle made to fit him.

She leaned back just enough so she could put his arms around his neck and draw him closer to her. Her lips on his were soft and perfect. He understood what she meant when she said he made her feel alive, because she made him feel the same way.

Then her tongue tickled against his. And he thought he was going to have undo his fly in order to be able to breathe.

He held her closer. He should never have kissed her.

Ending it was almost as hard as his dick. The kiss left them both breathing heavily. He cleared his throat. "Pancakes are ready."

Then anger clouded her expression. "If you're toying with me..."

"I'm not."

"Then stop riding a see-saw with me."

Anger filled her expression. Color deepened in her cheeks. He liked to think it was his kiss that did that.

"I'm not—" he tried again, but she interrupted.

"Yes, you are. You rip the rug out from under me by telling me about letters I never even knew about, and then you avoid me. Then you hold me in your arms. You tell me you plan to touch me, but you don't. After I pour my heart out to you, you suck it out with a kiss, but afterward you shove me away. If that's not a see-saw ride, I don't know what is. Decide right now and tell me how you want it. Either this is one hundred percent or it's zero. None of this back-and-forth shit. All or nothing."

Right then, he wanted more than all. He could have grabbed her, shoved her up against the planks of the barn wall and kissed her while he held her hands over her head and made love to her. He thought it would be easy enough. After all, he was certain she wore nothing under his shirt.

He met her gaze. Saw her need there—as strong as his felt. And he thought *why the hell am I punishing us? Why wait? Why waste any more time?*

He gave into that need. And kissed her again.

He didn't shove her up against the wall. He gently took her there, his kiss unending. He laced his fingers of one hand through those of one of hers and held tight, as if letting her go would be the end of him. He would have held onto her other hand, too, but he was busy using that one to undo his fly and get his jeans and red boxer briefs out of the way. Jee-zus his underwear had not felt this tight when he put them on after his shower a short time ago.

Finally.

Freedom. Sweet freedom. He felt like he could breathe as he let his jeans and underwear fall to the floor. All the while, he made love to her mouth with his. Kissing her was heaven to his soul, and she kissed him back with total abandon. She was shorter than he. He was stronger.

He lifted her up, raising his shirt she wore. Her stomach was smooth beneath his hand as he lifted that shirt out of the way. Her panties were lacy and nothing more than a sliver of material that covered her. His fingers of one hand brushed along her velvet flesh as he slid her panties down. Nothing else had ever felt so fine. She kicked them off, still kissing him.

Then they were both free, and she could wrap her perfect legs around his waist. He helped her. For the first time in weeks, his leg didn't burn with the morning. In fact, it didn't ache at all as he lifted her and easily maneuvered her into just the right place. He paused for a second, perhaps two.

"What are you waiting for?" Her question was breathy, her voice husky and seductive.

"Nothing."

He slid inside her.

And when he met resistance, he simply pushed through.

It wasn't until he felt her tense and heard her moan did he understand. It was too late.

He couldn't have stopped then if her father burst through the door. No, he was lost.

In her.

In the way she clung onto him.

In the way her heart beat with his, and her heat filled him.

In the way her kiss kept him from drowning.

In the way she fit him so perfectly.

In the way she made his world, his life, everything he knew complete.

Only then did the rest of his body join his lips and make love to her.

It was so much more than action, more than a mere thrust of his hips. It was an ancient dance that finished when their souls joined. When he climaxed and his moan was lost against the hollow of her throat, neither of them was reminded of Stan's fingers squeezing there. In fact, there was only the two of them as the rest of the world melted away in the heat of their moment.

Moments later—or was it hours? Perhaps weeks? He couldn't tell—he stood with her, still holding her, her breasts against his chest, her back against the wall. She was still snaked around him, holding tight. Now the fingers of both his hands were laced with hers over her head, and he couldn't remember moving to get there. He rested his forehead against hers and listened as together they panted. Their breaths were the only sounds in the room.

"You should have told me," he said softly. "I wouldn't have let it be so hot, hard, and fast. I would have been gentler or at least tried to be." He felt as if his words were a lie. He wasn't certain he could have.

"I didn't want you gentle. I just wanted you. You can be tender next time."

He would have questioned her more on the fact she was a twenty-nine-year-old virgin, but her *next time* stopped him in his tracks. As he thought about it, he didn't need to question her. He could tell all the work she put into the bakery. She poured her time into it. And her energy, neither of which she obviously put into any relationship.

Slowly, he lowered her to her feet, carefully. His jeans were still around his ankles. The last thing he needed, last thing his wounded thigh needed, was to trip on his own jeans and fall to the floor. He didn't want to explain that to his surgeon. "Did I hurt you?"

"I'm all right. Quit treating me like a doll that might break."

He also hoped to hell she didn't just let him do what he did so she could still wiggle it under anyone's nose. He didn't think that'd be true, considering she'd saved it all this time. Then he suppressed a shudder when he glanced down, saw blood on his dick.

She gasped. He lifted his gaze to her, expecting her to also be staring at the blood. Instead, she stared at the fresh scar on his thigh. "What the hell happened to your leg?"

It was time to be straight with her. He wanted this with her, this...

Whatever it was. A relationship? A path to something permanent where he could sleep with her in his arms every night? He didn't care what it was called, as long as he could have it. And he couldn't start with lies or withholding any information. He needed her to trust him.

Hell, he just plain needed her.

"Let's take a shower. Then I'll make some new pancakes and we can talk while we eat. I have a lot to tell you."

"If this is the same shower I used last night, I doubt we can both fit in there at the same time." Her hand was on his chest, as if she was afraid to stop touching him.

He liked that. With his fingertips, he tucked her hair behind her ear before he leaned down and picked up his underwear and jeans. "We'll make it work."

Chapter Fourteen

They did make it work.

"This is a pretty tight fit," she said.

Mac snuggled up against her back, hugged her to him from behind, and ran his hands over her breasts, spreading soapy bubbles. "You're a pretty tight fit, too."

She let out a sound that reminded him of the girl he knew in high school, the girl who had giggled in his arms when they danced.

"Do you want to know the second-best thing about squeezing into the shower like this?"

"What?"

"Neither of us can hog all the water."

She laughed again. "What's the first thing?"

"This." He rubbed against her and caressed her more.

"Mmm, you're right."

They showered until the hot water ran out, touching, exploring, sharing soapy caresses as well as kiss after kiss. A kiss on the lips, a kiss to a shoulder or the back of a hand. And Lizzy learned there was nothing more breathtaking than having him massage her scalp as he washed her hair.

Mac wanted to make love to her again. Under the hot water, their bodies covered with slippery suds. It would be so easy, so perfect. He held back. He wasn't even certain if she needed time to recover. He thought it best. Besides, he'd promised his dad he would help get ready for all the school kids coming today. At the rate he and Lizzy were moving, they might miss the show.

They dried one another, still stealing kisses, still caught up in touching here and there.

The moment felt magical, given the early sunlight coming in through the windows in warm rays. And he wished more than anything time could stop and they could just live this moment.

Unfortunately, Stan lurked outside somewhere, his father still expected his help, and the ghost of Kelly Mattis lingered over the entire town like a fog.

"So, tell me about your leg."

It was a half hour after the shower and they were finishing pancakes while he sipped coffee and she drank hers iced. He thought it wasn't anything close to the rich coffee she served in her bakery, but she didn't complain.

He should have known no matter how much he caressed her in the shower, she wasn't going to forget the question of what happened to him.

"I got shot," he replied. He knew it was blunt. He was blunt. There was no getting around what happened to him. There was no hiding what he was any longer. And he thought telling her he got shot was enough. He didn't feel it necessary to tell her he got shot twice.

She blinked at him as if she didn't understand his words. "What?"

He set his cup of coffee on the small table between them. The thud the action made seemed to echo across the loft room. Without a word he got up and opened the nearby nightstand drawer. He felt her gaze on him, warm and steady as he set his gun and his badge on the table in front of her before he sat back down again.

Her eyes were big green saucers. She stared at him for a long, silent moment before she hesitantly touched his badge with her index finger before she picked it up and studied it closer.

"Federal Bureau of Investigation?"

"Yep."

"That's where you've been for the past decade? Wearing a suit?"

He offered her a slight shrug. "I finished college first. For a little more than half a decade, I've been undercover, infiltrating biker gangs and big businesses. So, sometimes I have to wear a suit. Last month I was investigating a shrimp boat operation in the Gulf of Mexico. I thought it was drugs. Turned out it was sex trafficking. Women and children. I guess they didn't like my putting a wrench into their works."

"Oh, my God..."

He knew this was a lot to digest. He also knew this might be enough to scare her away or at least back to her bakery. He let out a breath of relief when she remained in her chair and didn't make a bee line to the door. "Do you have to worry about them coming after you?"

"No. Number one, I worked under a complete alias, looked a little different, too. Number two, as far as any of them know, they killed me. Number three, I worked it in such a way that it ended well for the victims. None of the shrimp need to be worried. At least not from that group."

"You got shot before it was over?"

"It got...intense."

He didn't want to scare her any more than necessary. And she obviously had been too caught up in the moment while he had his pants down and then too shocked by the scar on his leg that she didn't notice the second scar on his lower left abdomen. Intense was putting it lightly. If he hadn't had a few people on his side as well as the right people in the right places, he might have been floating at the bottom of the Gulf as fish food right now instead of sharing this moment with her.

"And now?"

"Now...I'm on leave, indefinitely, while I heal. I thought this would be the best place to do it. I knew about the picnic and the reunion," he paused and met her gaze. "That wasn't all."

"Oh?"

He gave her a small smile. "When you're lying on a gurney, bleeding, thinking you might not make it, you see your life from a whole new perspective."

"I'll bet. It's probably a lot like having someone with a hand on your throat."

"Probably. It's like what you said about what you want in your life."

"Is that what made you think about kissing me?"

"It made me think about a lot of things. The truth is, I saw a lot of unfinished business. I saw Kelly Mattis wearing a pink dress covered with blood. I saw my parents. I told myself I couldn't die. I couldn't let them learn about my getting killed via some phone call from some faceless person they didn't know. I also saw you, Lizzy. All these years, I've been in contact with your brother. I knew you weren't married. I couldn't die without seeing you. While I wasn't dreaming about you every night, I felt there things left unsaid, like unfinished business. You hated me and I needed to know why, needed to set that straight. I couldn't stand in that uncertain doorway any longer. I had to know why you never answered my letters. I couldn't die, and I couldn't live with so many unanswered questions anymore.

"So here I am. Back to take care of at least some of the unfinished business and get some answers. I just didn't have any idea how much business was here waiting for me."

Lizzy held up his badge, and then let it drop back to the table. It made a sound a lot like the thud his coffee mug had made. Without a word she stood. Her feet, still bare, were silent on the wood planks of the floor as she stepped to the sliding glass door at the far of the room where he'd sat with Tony. She only stared out and didn't open it.

Watching her back, he was glad she hadn't headed the other way to the door that led down out of the loft and out of the barn. He remained where he was, allowing her to accept all of his words. He knew it was in a nutshell, but for now, it had to be enough.

When she spoke, she did so as she stared out at the orchard, and he had the feeling she was talking more to herself than to him. "We were so young. And careless. You have no idea how many times I've wondered how different things would have been if we hadn't been parking by the tunnel, if we had gone to Lexi Harman's house for her after-dance party."

"Don't." He got up and closed the gap between them. With her back against his chest, he leaned closer, breathing in the soft scent of her hair. He put his hands on her arms and gently caressed her. "We can't change any of it. We can't go back, and it's stupid to even want to. We can only concentrate on what lies ahead for us. There is only now. We can plan for tomorrow, but we can only live now. If there is one thing I learned when I thought I might die it's that I don't want to waste any time. I don't want to waste another second at all." He gently cupped her face in his palm, forcing her first to look at him, and then pivot slightly to face him. "Not another second."

She sucked in a breath. Against his palm, she nodded. "Me, either. Not another second."

He held her close for several long, silent moments. "Are you ready to venture downstairs to help my parents deal with about a hundred little kids?"

The smile she gave him was quick but genuine before she nodded again. "Do you think your mom has a scarf I can wear?"

"I'm sure she has something that will work for you." He held her for another long moment, breathing past the way she fit so perfectly against him. The kiss he gave her was a bit more lingering than he planned. He was afraid to do too much, or his dad would be handling the first-graders alone. She waited while he strapped on his gun, slipped his badge into his pocket, and put on a jacket. He held her hand, needing to keep her as close to him as possible, as together they left the loft. It was a brilliant fall day that he thought was a beautiful new start for them.

Chapter Fifteen

Chief Franklin Daniels pinched the bridge of his nose between one thumb and index finger before he watched the sun rise. He took a gulp of coffee that was too hot. It burned his throat all the way down to his belly.

"You're still upset, Frank."

He closed his eyes, doing his best to ignore the sexy emphasis Kathleen Gresden put on each word. She always spoke to him like a purring sex kitten. Damn, the last thing he needed to think about was a kitten, any kitten. It reminded him of her stupid son and his craze of needing to strangle something in order to get off.

She tried to appease him as she always did, by undoing her blouse and showing him her glorious tits. The next thing he knew she straddled him as he sat on the kitchen chair. She rubbed against him like a cat needing attention, too.

He hated himself for having such a weakness when it came to her. He hated her more for acting on that weakness and taking advantage.

Not giving him a chance to reply to her question, she flattened her lips to his and forced her tongue into his mouth. It reminded him of the fantastic things she could do with that tongue, many of which she did just a few hours ago.

He allowed himself a few moments to enjoy kiss then, disgusted, he twisted away and out of reach. He told himself he was tired of playing games. No, the truth was, he was tired of *her* playing *him*. She'd been playing him for eleven long years. He thought it was time to pick up his toys and go home.

She tightened her thighs on his legs. "Oh, what's that I feel, so big and so hard, Frank? Is that your gun?" She leaned close and snaked her tongue up his neck beneath his ear, knowing damned well, that little subtle action would make him rock hard.

He tried to ignore it. Not possible.

"Stop," he let out, feeling like she sat on his chest and prevented him from breathing instead of sitting on his lap.

She wiggled her crotch against the bulge in his jeans. Damn her. "You don't really want me to stop."

"I need to get to work." He really needed to get away from her. It was as if she cast a spell on him. And ever since the first time he'd slept her—which he thought was heaven—he'd been in hell with all her blackmail.

"I could follow you, show up in your office ten minutes after you get there, and we could do it on your desk. Remember the last time we did that, remember how much you liked it?"

"I remember you've held it over my head for a long time."

He also remembered how she'd managed to have a little camera attached to her purse and caught it all on video. She told him she'd captured it all on video so she could relive the moment whenever she wanted to. Lying bitch.

"A girl's gotta use whatever bit of ammunition she can get her hands on."

He was amazed, actually, at how much *ammunition* she'd managed to accumulate on him. As he recalled, she'd jumped from beaten down victim, wife of an abuser, to a controlling monster in a matter of weeks. He literally bit his tongue to keep from pointing out to her she was no *girl*. He was pretty sure she had a line on her face for every time Randy Gresden hit her or slammed her up against the wall.

"Thanks to your son who can't keep from choking something or someone when he has one of his hands around his cock, things are just a little out of hand, wouldn't you agree?"

She slowly licked her lips while making certain he saw her lick them, and met his gaze with a very knowing grin. "Oh, I'm sure you'll figure out a way to fix everything. You always do." She held his hand for a second before she sucked on his middle finger.

He didn't know what got a hold on him, or where he found the courage, perhaps it was hidden in the woods outside Marston's Tunnel where he'd stood in the dark a few hours ago. All he thought was *no more,* he'd had enough. He yanked his finger from her mouth, ignoring the seductive pop sound that echoed through his kitchen. Then he stood up, dumping her off his lap and down onto the floor where she landed on her ass.

She tossed the fake-colored blond hair out of her face and jumped to her feet, snarling like a badger he'd once encountered on a hunting trip. "How dare you!"

He stuck to his guns. He didn't back down. He didn't even step back when she invaded his space. "Don't you understand? I don't know a way to fix this. I can help hide Stan, for a while, like you asked last night, but not for long. I'd bet my next paycheck Lizzy Signorino is going to be my office when I get there to formally charge him with assault. I can try to smooth it, but the truth is there is a recorded 9-1-1 call. There's Swornson as a witness." There was also a text on his phone from her asking for help. Damn her for that, too.

"And what a great witness Swornson is," she chimed in. "He likes his blow jobs as much as you do. Maybe more."

He ignored her. "There were pictures taken at the clinic. There are bruises on her throat. There are medical reports of the assault. This is no longer a he-said, she-said incident. This isn't a *Teacher, he pushed me down on the playground. Okay, say you're sorry. Now everything's good and normal* situation. If I try to sweep this under the rug and it backfires, he may end up in court trying to explain to a judge how he needs to jack off the way he does. And I could be standing right next to him. You could start by telling me what kind of drugs he's doing. We could get him some help."

The grin she gave him now was evil, pure uncontrolled evil. She shook her head in denial. "He doesn't need help."

Frank doubted that.

"You'd better figure out a way to make it a *normal* situation, Frank. Because if my boy goes down—ruined by that little slut who runs the bakery—then you go down, too. And I'm sure all of those grievances against Swornson that you've ignored the past year or two won't bode well on your record." She relaxed. Her features smoothed quickly, and she was once again the happy, good-morning, ray-of-sunshine woman so fast it was as if the hissing animal of a few seconds ago hadn't been there at all. "And, although I'd love to fuck you on your desk." She buttoned up her blouse before she checked her phone. "I have to get to work. I just remembered I have a field trip today. Doesn't that sound fun?"

She straightened her clothes and patted her hair. A few seconds later, she was gone, leaving without another touch or kiss, and the kitchen was blessedly quiet.

Frank sat back down on the chair with a heavy sigh. Fatigue gripped his bones, leaving him as though he'd just survived a tornado. As a younger man, he'd had such plans, so many ideals. How had he gotten here?

His phone signaled a text arriving. He contemplated ignoring it. He already knew who it was.

I could use some breakfast.

Her idiot son had no idea how much trouble he was in. He just figured he had the main cop in town wrapped around his little finger and that Frank was at his beck and call.

All because of one mistake. One mistake he could never fix.

He thought about texting back *fuck off* and letting the heads roll where they may.

In the end, he didn't. In the end, he picked up a breakfast sandwich and the largest cola that was offered at the fast-food drive thru and delivered it to Stan. He considered adding a box of rat poison to the soda.

Frank was already in hell. It wasn't like it would make matters worse.

****

Downstairs in the barn at the apple orchard, Lizzy discovered Robert and Ginna had set a long, but low-to-the-floor table with cups of apple cider. Large doors were open on all three sides of the barn, letting in sunshine and a nice fall breeze.

"Good morning," Ginna said as if Lizzy coming down from the loft with her son was nothing unusual.

She did her best to ignore the heat that crept into her face. "Good morning."

Mac's mom put her at ease. "We really appreciate your help this morning. I don't think Robert and I could take care of all the kids we expect today without your and James' help."

"I've probably got enough apple fritters at the bakery to cut up and serve if you'd like me to go get them," Lizzy offered.

"Tony already delivered them. That was so nice of him. I put them over there on the workbench counter with a knife and a few trays if you wouldn't mind cutting them into smaller pieces."

"Is it possible I could borrow a scarf, something to—" She carefully put her fingertips on her throat. "—cover this up? I didn't think to pack something."

Since Ginna didn't ask her what happened, Lizzy figured Mac had told his parents the entire story. "Of course. I'll be right back."

When Ginna stepped away, Lizzy plucked out her phone from her pocket and speed dialed her brother. In the middle of the second ring, he answered with, "Hey, how are you feeling this morning, Sis?"

"All right, I guess."

"You sure?"

"Yes...no...maybe."

She heard him let out a heavy breath. "Tiffany and I got things here, so just take a day off, a few if you need them."

"Tiffany's helping?"

"Yes. And Dane's coming when he gets off work. We'll get things ready for tomorrow."

"Thank you." While she liked the idea of a rest, it felt as if she wasn't really needed.

"You're welcome. You know I'd do anything for you. For now, stay with Mac."

It was what she wanted more than anything—to stay with Mac. The memory of him making love to her filled her with a river of warmth. "You knew he was FBI?"

"I did."

It was her turn to let out a huffy breath. "Did you happen to know Stan was into choking things while he..."

"No, that part was pretty much a secret."

Her next breath was a sigh of relief. "So, are there any other secrets I should know about?"

"Offhand, none I can think of."

"Thanks for delivering the apple fritters."

"Let me know if you need anything else."

She looked up. Ginna stood nearby holding a scarf. "I'll talk to you later."

"Keep me posted," he instructed. "And stay close to Mac. I mean it."

"I will."

"I love you."

"Love you, too."

A few moments later, she finished tying a fashionable gray scarf loosely around her neck before she picked up a knife to cut the apple fritters into pieces so there would be enough for all the kids. She smiled to find Mac's parents also had apple slices with cinnamon and sugar for any kids with food allergies.

It was good to have busy work. It took her mind off her throat and how she felt the need to hide it under a scarf. She realized then that Mac making love to her and sharing the shower with her had also distracted her enough that she didn't even think about studying it in the mirror.

She was just finishing cutting a tray of apple fritters when the first school bus arrived.

Being with the little kids was exactly what Lizzy needed. Seeing their excitement, witnessing their natural curiosity and wonder at its best as they tried to pick high apples, hearing their joyful chatter and squeals as they rode on the wagon Mac dragged with the tractor, kept her smiling. Riding on the wagon right behind Mac, watching his strong back as he maneuvered the tractor as if he'd been driving one all his life, and meeting his glances back at her were all part of their own secret communication.

After the second class of children finished filling their small bags with apples, they all sat down at the table which was now set with new paper cups and cut apple fritters. With a pitcher of apple cider in hand, Lizzy began filling cups while Robert gave a demonstration about the different types of apples and how when an apple is cut through the middle, the core resembles like a star.

"I didn't know you were out here lending a hand at the orchard."

She never considered she might see Stan's mother, Kathleen Gresden, today. It took a moment for her to remember the woman was a teacher at the grade school. "Oh, hi. That's right, you teach first grade."

"Yes." Kathleen stared at her for a long moment before she gave a quick glance to the scarf on Lizzy's neck. "So, what? You don't have enough to keep you busy at the bakery?"

Lizzy shrugged. "I had too many apple fritters, so I thought the kids could have a treat today."

"I see."

She couldn't help but wonder just what Kathleen could see. She wondered if Stan had shared with his mother what happened yesterday or if Kathleen even had a clue as to what Stan did with the cats in his shop. She decided it wasn't her place to share the secrets. "It's nice to see you, but I need to go and get ready for the next group of children. Robert and Ginna are trying to squeeze in all the classes due today before the rain comes in."

She took a tentative step away. She needed Mac, needed to know he was close, that she was safe.

Kathleen's next words made her pause. "You haven't seen Stan this morning, have you?"

"No, no I haven't." She didn't add that she hoped to never see him again.

"I guess you wouldn't see Stan if you got out here to the orchard *really* early this morning, and you weren't at the bakery." Kathleen's words were laced with sweet sugar, and she spoke them with a knowing ring in her voice.

"I guess not." Lizzy's jaws hurt from the smile she kept on her face. "*You* haven't seen Stan, have you?"

"No, I thought when he didn't come for taco night, maybe he was with you all night."

She shook her head. "No."

Stan's mother tossed her head slightly. "Oh, well, when you see him, you can tell him Elliot and his mama ate all the tacos."

"Sure." Lizzy didn't plan to tell Stan anything. She planned to stay as far away from him as possible. Maybe Stan disappeared and was hiding, and his mom didn't know a thing. The direct way Kathleen stared at her and smiled before sauntering off told her *mommy* knew more than she was saying.

A few moments later, Lizzy leaned against the fridge in the back room of the large barn. She feigned needing more apple cider in her pitcher. What she'd really needed was to breathe.

In that forced, sweet smile Kathleen had given, Lizzy saw Stan grinning at her, calling her a slut.

Breathe in. Breathe out. She closed her eyes, wishing she could close out the memory of the feel of Stan's hand cutting off her air. While Mac and the orchard had diverted the horror of that moment, it amazed her how easily it could slide back to the front row. It amazed her even more how it affected her, leaving her chest tight, her hands clammy, and the bitter, metallic taste in her mouth that burned her throat. She took a deep breath, determined not to let the episode control her.

"You okay?"

Mac startled her, made her jump and let out a gasp. She hated that, too. She never wanted to be afraid of him. His arms felt wonderful. Safe and perfect.

"I'm okay. I just...Stan's mom is out there."

"Oh, damn, I forgot she's a teacher."

"It's okay." He gently coerced her into his embrace. "I just needed a few minutes to catch my breath."

"Take all the time you need. And if you need to go upstairs and leave all this down here, feel free. I know it's going to take some time for you to get over what happened to you."

She relaxed in his arms and leaned into his embrace. He smelled of outdoors and apples. And Mac. Just Mac, like a cool evening in the woods. She took a deep breath, her chest feeling lighter.

"I'm feeling better already," she said. "With a little more fresh air before it starts to rain, I'll be good as new."

"I've got one more trip driving the tractor and hauling the wagon full of kids out into the orchard."

"That sounds like a ride I need to take."

He held her hand as they strolled toward the waiting tractor and wagon. Already, kids were piling on, finding places to sit while teachers and chaperones instructed them. Lizzy relaxed seeing no sign of Stan's mother. She raised her chin. Sunshine was warm on her face as she breathed in a deep breath and listened to all the sounds of normal. The laughter of children, birds singing, the rustle of the breeze through the trees. She breathed in deep again. The fresh air that smelled like apples was cleansing and warm and wonderful.

She could get over what happened with Stan, put it completely behind her.

And she would.

She leaned closer to Mac for a kiss. His mouth felt perfect on hers.

His kiss healed her heart like a tiny needle making stitches to keep the horror of Stan's action in the back of her mind where it needed to stay. She knew she'd get over this. She had a lot of support in the way of her family, her brother. She had friends. She had Mac and his parents. She had the business she worked to build. She just needed some time. And some patience. Mac helped her onto the wagon. Then he met her gaze before he climbed onto the tractor and checked his passengers.

"Everyone ready?"

All the little kids screamed out, "Yes!"

They headed toward the apple trees, the tractor puffing and chugging along, while the kids started singing about how the wheels of the tractor go round and round.

Mac stopped in the middle of the orchard. Kids scattered happily.

"Clouds are coming in," she said.

He studied up at the sky. "Yep, they better pick apples fast."

There were several, "Look at this one! It's the biggest!" And, "Oh, I stepped on a rotten one!" Or, "I got one more in my bag than you did!"

She stood next to the wagon and watched him as he spent the next several minutes helping a few of the children pick higher apples or again showing them how they should pick by turning the apple upside down.

"Are you doing all right?" he asked a short time later.

"Yes, much better. I just needed some fresh air. And to be here with you. Thank you for today. If I'd been in the bakery, I might have suffocated."

"You're welcome. This is the last load for today. Even though there may be customers who come out to pick, there aren't any more classes of kids until tomorrow.

Distant thunder rumbled. Mac directed his attention toward the kids and chaperones who were picking apples. Lizzy listened as he gave everyone instructions to pick up the pace so they could get back before it started raining.

The smell of approaching rain mingled with the scents of apples. The day was warm, but the breeze held a hint of blowing in cooler air as the warmth of the sun was disappearing behind dark clouds.

Lizzy fought back a shiver on the wagon ride back to the barn where buses waited to take the children back to school.

Amazing, she thought, as she contemplated all the changes in her life in the past three days. And to just think, less than a month ago, Stan had asked her what kind of engagement ring she'd like to wear forever on her finger. She had thought that romantic. If she'd left the bakery ten minutes later, she might never have seen this bad side of him. The cat might be dead. If Mac hadn't come to town, she might have been eating tacos with Stan, Elliot, and his mom, never even suspecting any of this. She might have married into this. Although she was sure she wouldn't have let things go that far with Stan.

She told herself she should be grateful. It was true she and Mac were moving fast, maybe too fast, but he'd obviously saved her from a lifetime of misery. Anyone, including her parents, would tell her to slow down, that she needed to get to know him. He was, after all, no longer that boy she remembered who danced with her. The truth was, she was certain her soul knew him. Her heart knew him. She wanted to spend the next sixty years getting to know him better.

Three days ago, she would never have believed she'd be here with Mac. But she was. Out of something so horrid, came something so wonderful.

She and Mac... She liked the idea of that. She had told him next time he could be gentle, and he was more than okay with the idea of a next time.

He stopped next to the barn. The kids were well behaved enough to follow the rule of waiting until they were excused to jump off the wagon. Mac climbed off the tractor and offered her a hand stepping off the wagon. She smiled down at him. Desire filled his gaze. She grinned, thinking he might as well have the words *I want you* stamped on his forehead.

Beside him, she watched the kids all head back onto the buses. Several choruses of "Thank you, Mr. McLane!" or "Thank you, Mrs. McLane!" rang out before they climbed onto the bus.

Lizzy watched his mom and dad and waved to the kids. "Your parents live for this. Look how much they love it."

"I know," his whisper was warm in her ear.

Lizzy took a deep breath of the clean, apple filled air. She knew they had to take this one day a time, but she couldn't help but wish time could stop right now, right here where she and Mac could stay in this perfect moment. She thought about what Mac said about stepping forward. She couldn't do that until she took care of things regarding Stan.

Ginna stepped away. "I'm going to go make us a late lunch." She smiled at Mac and Lizzy. "You two will eat with us, won't you? I can make some sandwiches and we could eat out here in the barn."

Lizzy smiled. "Sounds like a picnic. Thank you."

They watched her head into the house. Mac's dad headed toward the tractor. "Do you want me to put that away, Dad?"

"Thanks, but I got it." He climbed on. Before he started it, he shifted and gazed at Mac. "Hey have you seen Ozzie today?"

"No. Now that I think about it, I haven't."

"I think I'll take a ride around before I put it away and see if I see him." He started the engine and the tractor slowly chugged down the lane toward shed where equipment was stored.

"What are you thinking?" Mac asked, stepping closer to her.

"It's probably for the best that I file charges."

"Probably," he agreed.

She shivered again and molded against to him. "Cold?" he asked.

"Yes, and I didn't think to grab a jacket."

"My denim jacket is hanging on a hook up in the loft. Do you want me to get it for you?"

"Such a gentleman," she said, drawn to him even more. "Thank you, but I can get it. I'll be right back." She headed toward the stairs that led up to the loft apartment.

The loft apartment was darker and filled with shadows now that the sun was no longer shining. Lizzy, however, didn't need a light to find Mac's jacket which was just inside the door hanging on a hook. She slipped it on and held it around her, not so much because she was cold, but because she was comforted by smell of it, the masculine, clean woodsy smell of *him*.

She heard the distant sound of the tractor as she retraced her steps to the big open room of the barn, which was now empty of people. Although open with doors open on three sides, it was growing dark with the coming storm.

She followed the sound of the tractor to the far door to see where Mac or his dad were before she cleaned up some of the left-over paper cups from all the little apple pickers.

A flash of motion caught her attention off to her right.

She thought perhaps it was Mac. Before she could even comprehend, even see it was a person, he was on her. And he knew exactly how to grab her and hold her to keep her from fighting her way free.

Chapter Sixteen

"Don't…"

He dragged the word out, his breath hot in her ear. "Don't make a sound. Don't make a move. Don't try any of that Judo crap. Or I will…cut. Your. Face. Off. And then, I'll cut up Mac's mother. She's in the kitchen, making what looks to be really yummy sandwiches."

"Stan, please—"

The cold, sharp point of a blade poked her right cheek while with his other arm about her neck, he held her in a crushing hold. "After that, I'll pay a visit to that cute woman helping out your brother at the bakery today. What's her name? Tiffany? Funny how she and Tony seem really chummy. I can't help but wonder what her husband, Dane, thinks about that."

Her eyes watered. Icy terror clenched her stomach, and she felt instantly sick. She was almost certain a huge hand with claws for fingernails tightened around her lungs making breathing suddenly impossible as she tried to suck in a breath and barely managed a gasp.

On top of all the terror that gripped her, there was a tidal wave of disbelief. If anyone had told her last week that sweet, soft-spoken, napkin-folding Stan was really a raving lunatic bent on cutting her face off, she would never have believed it. And to be so bold as to threaten it in the barn owned by the former Chief of Police, he must be really desperate.

"Stan, don't do this. Let me go."

"I said don't make a sound."

Jabbing pain at the skin of her cheek where the blade poked her make his position clear. Cold terror snaked clear to the pit of her stomach. She bit her lip and tried to breathe while her heart raced painfully in her chest.

"Now you're going to do me a favor," he said.

"Why should I do you a favor?"

"Oh, Lizzy, can't you just be nice to me? Because if you don't, I'd have no choice but to hurt you. And hurt the people that are close to you."

No one threatens the people I love. "What do you want?"

"All you have to do is go to Chief Daniels and tell him everything that happened yesterday was just a misunderstanding."

Yeah, right. I suppose everything right now, including the knife thrust to my face, is a misunderstanding, too.

"You see, Lizzy, I need to be in the shop, working, putting food on the table for Elliot and my mom. With this little *misunderstanding* between us, I can't do that. Now I really don't want to have to hurt anyone, especially you. I really care about you. We could have been good together."

And how do you ever expect to let me go and walk away because I really am going to kill you as soon as I'm free?

"Without the shop and my work, I've got nothing left to lose. Now, I understand with Mac back in town, I've pretty well lost you. Of course, I think you and I both know I never really had you. Your heart has always been closed off, at least to everyone but McLane. Anyone with a brain and pair of eyes could see that. I must admit though it was kind of fun while it lasted. And let's face it, you are the light against my dark. With you as my girlfriend, no one ever saw anything beyond that or noticed anything about my odd fetishes. No one even thought I had any fetishes."

Antonio did.

"With you, I could be so normal."

Lizzy closed her eyes for three seconds, feeling her own heart beating, hearing the roar of blood rushing in her ears, wishing more than ever she could close her eyes to the horrific situation. She had to do something, something that wouldn't put anyone else in danger.

"You can let her go."

The sound of Mac's voice startled her, sent her heart racing faster, terrifying her to the point that, if there was a needle on a gauge, it would clearly be far into the red. At the same time, it sent a dose of relief skidding through her.

She didn't turn her head, didn't even breathe, despite her need to turn and see him. She shifted her gaze just enough to take him in. He was not far away, so terribly close that he would feel the sting of Stan's knife, if Stan decided to turn and lash out with it. He held his gun a few feet from the right side of Stan's head.

Oh my God...

Again, she couldn't breathe.

"Oh, Mac, my best friend since second grade, my co-football captain. Don't you just wish we could go back to high school? I caught almost every pass you threw my direction, didn't I? Those were the days."

The sickening sweet way he spoke sent her stomach doing a somersault. Lizzy swallowed against the bile that burned her throat.

"I said let her go."

The authority in Mac's voice was low, even, frightening. There was no way in hell she ever wanted to deal with the man behind that voice.

"Are you really going to shoot me over a sweet piece of fluff, an airhead woman who doesn't quite understand what she thinks she might have seen yesterday, a woman who obviously doesn't understand a man's needs?"

The sound of Mac drawing back the hammer of the gun he held was his reply. It sounded unusually loud as it echoed through the empty barn. Lizzy couldn't breathe. She closed her eyes again. She didn't want to watch this, couldn't bear to see what terrible thing might be coming.

Then she heard Robert McLane. His voice held the same ring of authority. "If he doesn't shoot you, I will."

Lizzy still held her breath. And the strangest thought passed through her mind. She'd gotten to make love with Mac and feel his hands on her body. She'd gotten to experience Mac...

Stan let out a heavy sigh and let her go.

Lizzy thought her knees would buckle. How she managed to stay on her feet, she had no idea. She felt something warm on her cheek. She felt strong hands move her several steps away.

Stan's voice. Calm, too calm, oddly wondering in tone. "Wow, handcuffs? Are you into that kinky stuff, Mac? Did he handcuff you to the bed, Lizzy? I sure didn't notice that when I sneaked up into the loft last night and watched the two of you sleeping together. It took almost a half box of sleep-aid to put that stupid dog of yours to sleep so he didn't try and bite my leg off."

Mac's voice, harsh but controlled. "You have the right..."

Nothing registered, nothing made sense. It was like a connect the dots picture with several numbers missing. There were only the cool breeze blowing through the barn and pitter patter of drops of rain that began hit the roof.

Chapter Seventeen

Mac stepped into the bakery where the air was heavy with the aromas of flour, yeast, and fruit. He stopped short at the sight of Tony sitting on a nearby table. Mac couldn't help but notice the way Lizzy's brother positioned himself in a strategic location. While he appeared relaxed, with his ankles crossed and resting on a nearby chair, he sat where he could see whomever entered through the front door and still keep an eye on his sister as she worked in the kitchen. Tony wasn't alone. At the far end of the room, Dane Kizer reshelved books, while Tiffany wiped down the counters.

Through the open kitchen door, Mac studied Lizzy for a long moment as she never paused in her routine. Either she ignored the bells over the door that signaled his arrival, or she never heard it. But then she was pretty intent in shaping what must have been a few dozen donuts on the table before her. "Has she kept busy like that all afternoon?"

"Yep," Tony replied. "She's made enough pies to take us clear into next month. I have no idea how many loaves of bread she's got rising. And we'll have to give away donuts in order to get rid of them all before they turn stale. I would have slipped one of the sedatives we got at the clinic into her drink to slow her down, but so far, she hasn't taken a drink of anything. Tell me that bastard's been locked up for the rest of his life."

"As of right now, he's in County. They'll hold him until he can be arraigned and stand before the judge, who will decide if he can be cut on bail or not."

Tiffany stepped up. "There's even a chance of that?"

Mac didn't like it any more than anyone else. "There's always a chance."

"Will the judge know he threatened her and others with a knife and cut her face?"

Mac heard the frustration Tony tried to keep buried. Mac felt the same thing. Every time he allowed himself to think about Stan holding a knife to Lizzy, a tornado of boiling fury cut a path of destruction through his gut.

"He'll know." He didn't tell them Stan had already retained the services of Stella Hendricks, Attorney at Law. She was known to be a piranha in the courtroom.

There was a lot more he didn't say just then. It all tumbled around in him, giving him a roller coaster ride of confusion that left him with little more than disturbing, unanswered questions. He'd had to pull rank, show his badge, and threaten to call in colleagues from the nearest FBI office to get Stan 'processed.'

Chief Daniels opposed him every step of the way and defended Stan in a manner that left him wondering if maybe the two were lovers. At least with Stan at the county lock-up and not in one of the two cells at the town department, he would not be let out before the appointed time.

Daniels simply wasn't to be trusted, and Mac had yet to see the reason.

"So, he's probably only going to be locked up for a day or two until he goes before the judge?" Dane asked.

"Even Daniels doesn't know this, so keep it mum for now, but as we speak, I'm waiting on a search warrant. Maybe we can find something that puts more evidence against him. Right now, he can say he was distraught at knowing 'his girlfriend' was with another man. Me. Which also isn't going to help my case against him. And, since it's a conflict of interest, I thought it best to call in a few non-biased colleagues. So, they are now sifting through things and they'll be taking over."

"I see your point. That's probably for the best." Tony shook his head. "What do you think you—or they—might find with your search warrant? And what made you even think to try for one?"

"He threatened her with a knife."

Tony made the instant connection. "Kelly Mattis."

"Yeah."

"What motive could he have had?" Tiffany asked.

Mac could think of a few and took at step toward the kitchen. "Maybe she caught him strangling her cat. I'd also guess drugs are involved. If he can't be held on the assault charge, maybe he will on a drug charge."

"By the way, I tracked down Wellsburg and Hattersfield for you," Tony said. "Wellsburg is working in a department store in the Mall of America in Minnesota. Hattersfield has a job with the Postal Service and is delivering mail in Kansas City. I meant to tell you sooner, but other things seemed to get in the way."

"What about Stan's dad?" Mac was afraid to ask.

"No sign of him anywhere, but I'll keep digging."

He took another step toward the kitchen. "Thanks."

"I would advise you not to go in there." Tony got up from his seat and stepped in Mac's path. "My sister's not very *receptive* right now. In case you've never noticed, she has a little of our father's temper, stubbornness, and disposition."

"I never noticed that," Mac lied.

"Uh huh," Tony put in lightly as if he believed it. He didn't try to stop Mac a second time.

When Lizzy didn't acknowledge him, didn't stop twisting dough, he said, "How are you?"

"I'm just ducky. How are you?"

He thought she sounded a little slap happy, but he didn't comment on it. "Not even close to ducky."

"Mmmm, bad day at the office?"

"I'd say it was pretty bad."

"Maybe you should find a new office."

"I don't know about that, but we'll see what comes of it."

"Did you have to get a stitch in your cheek?" She continued to twist dough into coils.

"No."

"Anyone threaten you with a knife?"

He considered answering yes, because now that he thought about it, any threat to her was a definite threat to him. "No."

"Then I don't think your day was as bad as mine." She paused, met his gaze evenly, and offered him a smile that was forced and obviously as sweet as the sugar she used to sprinkle on her pastry. Then she was back at expertly twisting the next batch.

He thought about disagreeing with her. Watching it happen and not being able to stop it without his gun was no cake walk, either.

They were both quiet for a long moment. He watched her, not knowing what to expect. He remembered well the quiet way her father spoke to him through what was obviously fear and anger. A melt down? A screaming fit? Crying on his shoulder? Hell, he didn't really care. He knew she'd been terrified. He knew from his own experience she was going to have to let it out some way, somehow. And he wanted to be there to catch her and hold her when it happened.

She paused in her dough twisting, but stared down at her work. "Would you really have shot him?"

"Yes."

"Have you ever shot anyone before?"

"I'm not proud of having to do it, but yes." He didn't feel now was the time to tell her the man he'd shot and killed was the man who had shot him.

"Why is this happening? Why didn't I know?"

He wondered when she would question today. He knew she'd blame herself. "None of this is your fault."

"I've spent a lot of time with him. I've known him since grade school. I should have known. I should have recognized some sign. I should have seen something." She met his gaze. Finally. For longer than to just give him a phony smile. And he made sure she saw he wasn't looking at her. "What are you looking at?" She turned and followed his gaze over her shoulder.

"That wall behind you."

"What about it?"

"I haven't made love to you up against that one. Not yet. I thought we could make that one next."

She blinked at him as if she didn't comprehend what he was saying. After the day she'd had—her life threatened, a cut on her face when Stan touched the knife to it just before letting her go, hours keeping her hands busy with baked goods, she probably didn't. The shift in conversation was too swift, too sudden for her to keep up. It was what he wanted. It would help get a reaction from her. And he did get one.

"I should have known!"

Mac forced calm into his voice. "I've known him almost his entire life, I even knew about his OCD and needing to keep things stacked so neat. I let him stay at my house every time his old man was on the rampage, and I didn't know about any of this either."

"Yeah, well, you've been gone for a while remember?"

She still needed to blame someone or something to put things into some sort of perspective. He took another step closer. "I'm here now."

"I still should have known!" Her raised voice echoed through the kitchen.

"No one knew. Bad guys go to great lengths to keep all their secrets hidden in the dark so no one knows."

"He drugged your parents' dog!"

"Ozzie's fine. He's just a little dopey for now. He'll probably be back to his usual self and chasing rabbits tomorrow." Mac didn't point out that he thought Stan had taken a few drugs himself.

"Then you left me!"

"Yes, I did. For a reason," he explained with more patience than he felt. "I left you with Tony. Your brother. Your twin. I had to make sure

Daniels didn't turn around and send Stan home after a harsh talking to like an unruly schoolboy."

"I thought...I thought..." Now she was talking, no longer screaming, but at least trying to put some calm in her voice.

He gathered her into his arms. She held on to him, his shirt clutched in her fists. "I thought I was going to die. I didn't know what to do. I kept weighing—should I fight? Should I not fight? Then he threatened your mom and Tiffany and said he'd go after people I loved. I couldn't breathe. I couldn't think. I was terrified and angry at the same time."

She sounded liked she still was.

"Why did he do that to me? What does he have against women?"

He held her tighter. He had given up long ago searching for reasons why people do the things they do. It was just his job to stop them, not fix them. "Something he obviously learned from his father. And he did it because he thought it was his only way out of the situation. Desperate people do desperate things."

Not that he ever wanted another bad day. And he hoped beyond all hope to never again see anyone threatening Lizzy in any way. Through it all, he knew now the cure for a bad day.

To have her in his arms, where she was safe, where his heart beat with hers.

The world felt right when Lizzy was in his arms.

****

Mac stared at the smooth, soft-as-velvet skin of Lizzy's back while he caressed his hands across it. Concentrating on the sweet feel of her, he was able to keep his breathing under control.

At his direction, finally, she lay on her belly, her breasts hidden as he massaged her back.

He *attempted* to massage her back. It wasn't easy. Today she wore underwear that reminded him of his boxer briefs. How those could be so sexy, he had no idea. Of course, maybe it was the way they just hugged her shapely butt.

Her loft apartment above the bakery was filled with country things and white washed furniture and even one of those barn doors on a track, but he hadn't given himself much opportunity to really study it. It took all his energy to coax her into what he thought would be a relaxing massage.

And touching her, and seeing her in those sweet panties, left him far from relaxed.

He breathed, tried to calm his insides. The last thing he wanted her to feel was his tenseness or his lingering fury. This was for her. She needed this.

"Do you think he'll come back and try to hurt me or anyone else?"

He'd better not. "Try not to think about it." Mac circled his palms at her shoulder blades. "Just feel my touch." He forced himself to breathe easy.

She was quiet for a long moment.

He continued to study her skin as if she was a fine work of art—which he thought she was—as he worked his fingertips near her neck where he felt tension linger.

"I think I forgot to turn off the ovens downstairs."

"No, you didn't."

"Did I lock the door downstairs?"

"I did. Everything's fine. Now relax." Her fair skin was smooth, lovely. He could spend days just touching her.

"I should have run the dishwasher."

Damn, she was stubborn. Maybe he should have lit some candles or something. He was not about to take his hands off of her. Number one, he didn't want to. Number two, he was afraid if he did, she'd jump off the bed and be back downstairs making a cake or something. After all, he'd had to start with a rub of her shoulders and more or less trick her into getting her shirt and bra off just to get her into this position. It hadn't been easy. And he'd really thought he was going to have to hold her down and force a sedative down her throat. "Be quiet."

"I could turn over. You could make love to me. I liked making love with you."

He sucked in a breath, closed his eyes against that one, and deeply massaged his thumbs into a knot he felt in her upper back. "I *am* making love to you. With my hands. Enjoy it. Now no more talking."

"But you'll make love to me again with your lips and your..." She took a deep breath and yawned.

Finally, he thought. She was finally shutting down. He knew she was going on fumes of adrenaline. She needed rest. She needed sleep. He was surprised she hadn't crashed before now. "Yes. I'll make love to you again. With all of me," he said softly. Oh, yes, he planned to make love to her again. And again. And again.

"Promise?"

"I promise."

"Tomorrow?"

"Yes." Although he wasn't sure he could wait that long, especially if she didn't shut up.

"Promise?" Her single word sounded fuzzy and sleepy.

"I promise. Now just relax." He worked her back muscles with his fingertips. She smelled of flour and cookie dough. He fought the urge to lean over and put his lips or his tongue on the back of her neck to see if she tasted like cookie dough, too. He had to keep reminding himself he was trying to help her sleep—which she obviously needed—not stir her up.

"You'll be here when I wake up."

"Absolutely."

After another long sigh, her breath became rhythmic and even.

Mac never took his attention from her. For another fifteen minutes, he enjoyed touching her. The sweet feel of her back, the warmth that penetrated his arms and coursed through his body like an electric current, the perfect curve of her waist—he took it all in and memorized it like an artist.

And only when he was certain she was fast asleep did he carefully slide away, covering her with the quilt on her bed before he let the cold spray of her shower douse the fire she set in his soul.

Then, for the second night in a row, he slept with her in snuggled against him in his arms. He was pretty certain he would never again be able to sleep without her beside him.

Chapter Eighteen

Thursday

Chief Franklin Daniels sat in his office and tried—miserably—to breathe.

Breathe in. Breathe out.

Thinking about it was the only way to accomplish it.

Former Chief McLane's son was an FBI agent. To say that knowledge almost blew him off his chair was an understatement. Stan Gresden, that stupid prick, was in the county lock-up and Kathleen, damn her, was texting him.

Could things get any worse?

Two of Agent McLane's colleagues—Thompson and Pickering, both *personal friends* of McLane— just left his office, search warrant in hand. So yes, it was worse. His phone buzzed with yet another text.

What do you mean Stan was taken to County? You'd better do something. And fast. You'd better fucking answer me.

He wished he had a dollar for every time he considered and/or planned to kill her. He could buy an island somewhere and disappear. Let her find out the hard way the FBI was heading to her house with a warrant. He wished he could be a fly on the wall for that one. He was certain she'd offer to suck one of them off in order to hold them back.

Instead, he drew his police-issue revolver from his holster on his belt.

This wasn't how he'd planned his life. This wasn't how he'd planned to end it, either. He always thought if he was going to die on the job, he should go out in a blaze of glory, working to save others like a real hero. Perhaps he should have been a fireman, so he could have died in a fire saving a baby.

He should write a note. Clear up everything. Clear the air, as his mom used to say. He should check out with a clean slate.

Then again, perhaps he shouldn't take the time to write a note. He should just count. And get the deed done. It would end everything. It had to be easier.

One.

Two. He pulled back the hammer. The sound of it broke through the silent office like a firecracker.

He closed his eyes. And saw freedom. It was so close, like a light at the end of the tunnel of hell. Perhaps a light at the end of Marston's Tunnel.

"Excuse me, Chief."

Daniels let out his breath in a whoosh and lowered his gun to his side down below the desk where, Stella, the department secretary couldn't see it. Then he bit his tongue to keep from letting out the oath that almost slipped. "Yes, what is it, Stella?"

Divine intervention?

"You all right, Chief? You're a bit pale."

"I didn't sleep very well. Thanks for asking. What is it?" He forced out. Another second and the pretty blonde would be staring at his brains on the wall behind him. He swallowed through a tight throat and made certain his finger was off the trigger as he sucked in a deep breath.

"Officer Swornson. Again. There's been another complaint. Agnes Moore says she wanted to make out a report, an *official* report. She says he stopped her over last night when she was on her way home from babysitting for her daughter's kids, that he—and I quote—asked her to get out of her car before he rubbed his hand over her private woman parts and told her he wouldn't give her a speeding ticket if she got down on her knees like a good girl."

"Geez Louise! Has everyone in this damned town lost their mind?"

What he really thought was Swornson must be hard up to have to grope a woman like Agnes Moore. She had a face a lot like a horse and was almost as big as one. She was at least a decade and a half older than him and should ask permission before she wore any more spandex.

Stella shrugged as if none of this was news to her. "Maybe."

He met her gaze and wondered why he'd never been able to catch a woman like her. Smart, classy, wore clothes to work that were professional and pretty at the same time. She reminded him of an appliance poster advertisement model from the 1950s, and she did not have to ask permission to wear spandex. She kept her cool. Always. And she didn't seem the type who would give him a blow job and then blackmail him with video of it.

He was suddenly shamed at the idea he almost ate his gun for breakfast. He didn't want Stella to see him like that. In that single heartbeat, his gaze caught—was trapped—in hers, he vowed to change things in his town and in his life. He was setting things right, even if he had to pay for them. He was tired of his soul being eaten away a little piece at a time.

Starting right now.

"Where's Swornson now?"

"I would assume at home. His shift ended at midnight. Agnes Moore waited until now to report him because she wanted to make sure you were here."

He still held her gaze. "Do you think I should just fire his ass, or fill out the paperwork for administrative leave?"

She didn't pause to think about it. "If you just fire him, he's free to work somewhere else with no record of it. And he'll just grope other women. If you investigate him, involve others, have it on record with an administrative leave, he'll be charged. He needs to be stopped."

"Has he ever touched you, Stella?"

To his dismay, she didn't answer his question, at least not directly. "See that he's charged, Chief."

"Get me the paperwork." He watched her sweet, perfect backside as she stepped back to her desk. As soon as she was gone, Daniels slipped his gun back into the holster and secured it. Maybe he should put everyone out of their misery and just shoot Swornson. It was the surefire way to keep all the women of Mossy Point safe. And, given his week, he was certainly in the mood to do so.

He grabbed his phone with plans to speed dial the former chief, Robert McLane.

He saw a text before he could tap the right buttons to call the former chief.

The FBI is here. Where are you? I need your help. Get here fast. You know what happens if you don't.

He didn't reply.

Chapter Nineteen

"Franklin Daniels wants to meet with us."

Mac stared at his father. The orchard kept him busy in the mornings. And he liked Ginna's coffee. Except to buy a cake for a special occasion, Mac doubted his dad ever stepped into the bakery. Yet, here he stood at the counter. At least he hadn't come knocking while they were still up in Lizzy's loft apartment.

Mac had promised her they would make love again today. And he'd wanted to. Then when he woke with her in his arms, he'd been happy to hold her. Just hold her.

Not that it lasted long anyway. As soon as she noticed the time, Lizzy jumped out of his arms with, "Oh, my God, is that the time! I need to open!"

And nothing he said could coax her back to bed. So, he vowed to make it up to her tonight. Maybe he really would constrain her against that wall in her kitchen and make love to her. Then he thought he might just lift her onto the counter and enjoy a little tasty pie of his own.

Hardly two minutes after she flipped the open sign and unlocked the door, his father had hurried in.

Robert's words surprised him even more than his appearance did. "What? Why would Chief Daniels want to meet with us?"

Robert shrugged. "I have no idea. He called me, said he needed me at the station right away and he wanted you there, too. About thirty seconds after he called, Stella, the station receptionist called and told me she thought Daniels had been about to eat a bullet in his office and that she interrupted him. She's worried about him."

Mac looked at Lizzy. The dark circles under her eyes tugged at his heart. This was taking a toll on her. At first, he thought he was causing the problems. His return to Mossy Point certainly stirred up a hornet's nest. Then he reminded himself—Tony reminded him, too—none of this was his fault. The positive thing was he was here to hold Lizzy through it.

Lizzy stood behind the counter with a coffee pot in one hand.

"You can come with us," Mac suggested. "Or you can go out to the orchard with my mom." As soon as the words were out, he remembered what happened yesterday at the orchard. He had to remind himself Lizzy and his mom were safe with Stan locked up.

"Are you kidding? I can't just close up shop and leave. It's okay. Go ahead. I'll be fine."

"Are you sure?" He didn't believe the small smile she gave him was real.

"Tony will be back in an hour or two. I'll be in here with customers. I'll just keep giving out all the donuts I made last night. I think I'll even put a FREE sign on the little self-standing sign outside. That should keep the crowd in here." She put a few donuts into a bag. "Here, take these with you."

"And here, put my number in your cell," he instructed.

They spent the next few moments swapping numbers. Mac didn't feel good about leaving her, but it was better than nothing. "I'll be back as soon as I can. I promise." His kiss was quick but hesitant. He knew her fear was still raw. It didn't matter that Stan was in jail. The uncertainty of the situation was just as terrifying as Stan holding a knife to her face. And, of course, she was obviously reminded every time she spoke or smiled and her movement tugged against the stitch in her cheek. It also didn't help that everyone who ordered a cup of coffee thus far asked her what happened.

"I'll be waiting with coffee and more donuts. I have plenty of donuts."

He smiled at her lighthearted joke. "I'll be back as soon as I can." Then he headed out with his father.

The Mossy Point Police Station hadn't changed much since the last time he was there. The night Kelly Mattis was killed.

The only change was the name on the office where his father used to sit. Oh, and the receptionist was new, too. She was a real knockout. He wondered how Swornson, who seemed to need to swap sex for tickets, handled himself around that classy lady in a sweet pair of wide-legged pants and high heels.

Chief Daniels stood at the door to his office, waiting for them. He ushered them in and invited them both to sit. "Stella, would you mind getting us all some coffee?"

"I'd be glad to," the knockout receptionist replied, saying it in a way that told Mac she knew what Daniels needed to discuss and was eager to help.

Mac set the small bag on Daniels's desk. "Lizzy Signorino sent you some donuts."

"Oh, thanks."

Mac noticed he didn't grab the bag to check them out or eat one.

A moment later, Stella carried in a tray that held three cups of coffee poured into heavy ceramic mugs. All three of them refused sugar or creamer. Daniels waited for her to close the door before he said a word.

Saying nothing, Mac watched his dad carefully. He wondered if Robert ever sat on this side of the desk before now and how hard it must be for him to do so. He also knew this had to be important, or Daniels wouldn't have summoned them both.

"Would you care to tell us what this is about?" Robert asked. His voice was laced with frustration and indicated to Mac he didn't care to sit on this side of the desk. He probably had more school kids coming today and didn't have time for this.

"Before we get started, I want you to know I've started the paperwork to put Swornson on administrative leave. The only thing I need to decide is whether I should make it paid leave or not. I've let this go on a long time, and I'm not even sure why. I guess I've always felt sorry for him and I hoped he'd listen to me and follow a better path. So far, that isn't to be."

"Did you need help with the paperwork or something?" Robert remarked.

Yes, sitting on his side of the desk was eating at him, Mac thought with a mental grin, as he swallowed a drink of bitter brew that burned his throat.

"If you're bored and need something to do, that'd be great. I had no idea how much damned paperwork was involved." Daniels paused. "The truth is, I called you here because I have some confessions."

"Do you need us to call you a priest?" Robert asked.

Daniels met Robert's gaze directly. "I'm telling you because I trust you, because I know whatever needs to be done regarding them, you'll see it gets done." He shifted his attention to Mac. "I'm telling you because you're FBI and, because if something needs to be done that your dad doesn't have authority to get done, you can."

Mac met his father's gaze for a moment and noticed Robert hadn't taken any sips of his coffee, but had his attention on Daniels.

"This has to do with Kelly Mattis."

Mac's heart skipped and he forced his hand holding the mug of coffee to remain steady. What was Daniels going to do? Confess to killing her? Mac didn't think they could get that lucky after all this time. Besides, he was pretty certain his dad had questioned everyone in a hundred-mile radius of town after Kelly was murdered.

"I had sex with her." Daniels spoke without blinking an eye.

The room was silent for a long moment.

"Kelly Mattis?" Mac asked after he cleared his throat.

"Yes, Kelly Mattis."

"I'm not surprised, Chief," Mac said. "I hope you practiced safe sex because I think every guy in my class had sex with her."

"I meant about an hour or two before she was killed. So, what does that make me? Last, but not least?"

Now that shined a new light on the situation. Mac found his dad staring at Daniels with concern. Both of them set their coffee on the desk as if neither of them trusted themselves to hold it any longer. Mac licked his lips, but it didn't help his dry mouth, and then he faced Daniels again. "Did you kill her?"

"Hell no."

"Then I don't care that you had sex with her," Mac put in.

"She called me from the dance, asked me to pick her up."

"What time was this?" Mac interrupted.

"About nine o'clock."

"There weren't any calls on her phone." It was Robert's turn to interrupt. "I checked."

"Maybe she called from the pay phone or from a friend's phone. I don't know. She never called me on her own cell anyway. She said her parents checked her phone all the time. I don't remember the number that was used. I wouldn't have cared back then, or even given it much thought. I don't even know if you can go back that far in my phone records. I only know she called and I answered."

"Why'd she want you to pick her up?"

"She was upset. She wouldn't tell me exactly why."

"Probably because I was with Lizzy Signorino at the dance when Kelly thought I'd be taking her. Did she mention that?"

"No," Daniels replied. "But she sure had the hots for you."

He shrugged. He didn't care, besides Tony said as much.

"She said you were the only guy she really loved, but that you weren't interested. She said you were the only guy she'd ever given head to that was clearly distracted."

Mac supposed if his dad had to hear anything at all about it, that wasn't bad. "Does this have anything to do with who might have killed her?" He glanced at his phone. "Because if it doesn't, I want to get back to Lizzy."

Daniels continued, "We parked out the other side of the tunnel." He leaned forward and rested his chin in the palm of his hand. "From where you were later. We had sex in my car, with her sitting on my lap. We'd been having sex for a year. I know I was older than she was, but she made me feel...I don't know, important. I treated her like my girlfriend. Then that night I learned about all the others. I told her how I wished I could have taken her to the dance. She laughed in my face, said the last thing she needed was to be seen with me. She also told me she only kept me around because I was a better lay than some of the other guys she knew. A more mature lover, someone who knew what I was doing instead of the—and I quote—fumbling teenagers she usually had to deal with. I was really mad. She'd just straddled my lap, and I learned it'd meant nothing to her."

Again, the room was quiet for a long moment.

"*Why* are you telling us this now?" Robert asked.

Daniels scratched his head and shifted in his chair. "Kathleen Gresden knew I was seeing her, said she saw me pick her up from the dance, said she followed me and knew I took Kelly parking at the tunnel. She also said she saw Kelly hiking home later. She's been kind of blackmailing me since."

"*Kind of?*" Mac let out.

"It seems I screwed my way from one manipulative blackmailing bitch to another. I knew about that stupid son of hers, choking animals. I think he even killed a cat or two. I know the Drakes, who live behind the auto body shop had a litter of puppies earlier this year and found two out of the six dead, but I couldn't place Stan Gresden there. However, I also found evidence in the woods near the tunnel that he—or someone—was killing small animals. I didn't exactly overlook it. I tried to talk to him about it. I suggested some places where I thought he could get help. I guess he never took my advice, or it didn't work for him. Or perhaps Kathleen didn't think he needed it. She always justified everything either Stan or Elliot did. Not that it matters.

I helped her hide him last night. Kathleen has made it clear on every occasion she is determined to keep her boys safe from anyone who would want to even cause either of them pain. It's probably driving a stake through her heart with the idea he's up at County in Lock-Up. The truth of the matter is, I'm tired of carrying around the weight of Kelly Mattis, and Kathleen Gresden has been an exhausting see-saw ride that I can't handle anymore. Hell, I can't even say no to buying her a cup of coffee in Lizzy's shop, or she threatens to report me and expose me to the newspaper office."

He paused and shifted his gaze from Mac to his father, then back to Mac. "I needed to come clean."

Mac's thoughts were swirling like water going down a drain. He didn't even know if any of this information was helpful. It took a lot to digest it all. "How was Kelly Mattis when you were with her, besides upset about me?"

Daniels shrugged. "What do you mean?"

"Pre-occupied? Worried? Her usual self?" Mac specified. "Did she say anything about perhaps being followed or threatened?"

Daniels offered a lop-sided grin. "No, she didn't say anything negative. She was just...pissy. I think she needed the sex to let off steam. Her usual self was always pre-occupied. I'm sure in this day and age, the girl would have a label of ADHD or something equivalent. At the very least, she was spoiled. After we had sex, she asked me for money, which also wasn't unusual. I gave her a hundred dollars. I told her as soon as she graduated from high school, I wanted to date her for real. She laughed and said as soon as she graduated from high school, she planned to be out of this quote-unquote nothing town. I told her I wanted to marry her. She told me I was good enough to fuck, but not good enough to marry. She said if I didn't give her five hundred dollars, she was going to report me, that it would be statutory rape. She was seventeen. I was almost twenty-four I guess it finally hit just how much she used me, and how she thought she would continue to do so. I told her to get the hell out of my car."

Daniels stopped and shook his head as if doing so would shake away the memory. "I didn't have the money. I was trying to work my way through the police academy. When I told her that, she yelled at me, told me to go to hell. We weren't far from Marston's Tunnel. All these years, I've been haunted by the idea of how she loathed and pitied me, how she laughed as if everything we'd had for the entire year had been nothing but a joke. Then she climbed out and left. And obviously walked right into the arms of a murderer. Maybe if I'd kept her in my car another ten minutes, if I hadn't told her I wanted to marry her or even if I had told her I'd take her to get some of the money, she'd still be alive. I've spent the last eleven years working to give positive to this town, do whatever it takes to keep the town safe, and give everyone a positive change to stay on the right path. This is another reason I wasn't quick to arrest Stan or fire Jake. I was hoping I could get them on the right path. After this week of complaints against Jake and with what happened with Lizzy, I have no choice but to do something more, no matter how guilty I feel about not keeping Kelly safe."

The sound of a phone ringing filtered in from the outer office. With the door shut, it was muffled and was obviously answered by Stella since it only rang one time.

Mac well understood the guilt. He held no love for Kelly Mattis. If he had a dollar for every time he wondered if he'd even danced one dance with her at the dance, maybe it might have changed the night's outcome, he'd be a rich man and could retire tomorrow.

"You didn't see anyone else around or see which direction she headed when she left you?" Robert asked.

"No. I sat there for a few minutes, wallowing in my own self-loathing over how I'd been wishing for a life with her when I was nothing to her. When I searched around, I didn't see her. I purposely went the other way when I left and ended up at the Streetside Bar. I stayed until Jerry kicked me out at two. I didn't want to be at home alone. And if she considered going to my place, which I'm pretty sure she probably didn't, I didn't want her to find me there. I thought she deserved to find her own way home in those spiked shoes she was wearing. The next morning, my head pounding with a hangover, before I learned she was dead, I felt guilty because I remembered she had a sleeveless dress and no jacket and it was a cool night. At least I thought it probably was. I drank, hoping to forget. And it worked to a certain degree. I felt bad she was probably cold. I admit when I first heard she was dead which was later the next afternoon, I thought perhaps she'd stumbled down the embankment in those heels and broke her neck. Or fell because of her heels and froze. I had to tell myself it wasn't *that* cold. I was shocked as shit to hear she was...like that in the tunnel."

"Did you happen to give her a bracelet?" Mac asked, even though he knew Daniels had not been in metals class—at least not for a few years. The single sip of coffee he'd had now seemed to churn and boil in his stomach and he wasn't even sure why. Nothing Daniels told them led them in any direction or answered any questions.

"A bracelet? No. I'd bought her a pair of diamond earrings about, oh, I don't know, maybe six months earlier, and I'd had to take them back." He paused and chuckled bitterly. "Hell, I'd saved three paychecks to buy them, and she said she was allergic. I never bought jewelry again. Besides, all she really wanted was the money."

"How much did you give her? Total." He had his phone on vibrate and felt the buzz of it as a call came through. He ignored the call, uncertain if he was making headway in the cold case of Kelly Mattis or not.

Daniels let out a heavy breath as he thought about it. "Probably a few thousand dollars when it was all said and done. I have to admit, I didn't keep track. Fifty bucks here. A hundred there. Twenty if it was all I had in my pocket."

"You said you ended up at the Streetside after she left you?"

"Yep. I would venture everyone there could vouch for me. Her murder is like an omen. It seems like everyone remembers exactly where he or she was when *it* happened."

That was true. What everyone was doing when *it* happened always was a hot topic.

"So, if you feel you need to arrest me for having sex with a minor, then so be it." Daniels looked at Robert.

Robert slowly shook his head. "I'm not a cop anymore. I'm not going to arrest you."

Daniels gazed at Mac, too. Before Mac could reply, his phone buzzed again with an incoming call. Mac finally ventured an absent glance at the display. "I'll have to postpone arresting you, too, Chief. It's my colleague, Pickering, calling. Maybe they found something."

He couldn't help but notice the previous call had been Lizzy. A wave of guilt was nearly strong enough to sweep him off his feet. She'd dealt with so much since his return to the Point. He should have taken a moment to answer and make sure she was doing all right. He planned to call her right back.

He answered his phone with, "Yes, Liam?"

"We found nothing substantial searching the Gresden residence."

Mac felt his stomach drop. He needed something to keep Stan away from Lizzy. With a good lawyer, Stan could probably get out with a slap on the hand with an assault charge. Hell.

"You need to get to the storage unit Kathleen Gresden rents. You aren't going to believe what we found there."

"What?"

"Just get here. You need to see it." Pickering disconnected before Mac could question more.

Mac slipped his phone back into his pocket. "It sounds like the search revealed something."

****

Mac drove his dad to Kennedy Storage units on the north side of town.

He stopped at a stretch of yellow caution tape that was across the entrance of the row of units where he knew Kathleen Gresden's unit was. After all, he remembered seeing Kathleen at Kennedy's Storage the same night he saw Lizzy.

One of his fellow agents had stretched yellow caution tape at the opposite end of the row as well. He and his father climbed out and he held the tape up while his dad stooped under. Daniels parked next to his truck and joined them. He and Daniels followed Robert after they both bent under the tape.

The large garage door of one unit was open. All three of them stopped just at the entrance as if they were fearful of entering the shadowed area. There were a few boxes and several pieces of furniture in the unit. Red Christmas tinsel poked out of one of the boxes as if trying to escape.

At the far end was a large chest freezer, the lid open.

Mac's two colleagues, friends with whom Mac had sifted through debris searching for clues on more than one occasion, stood nearby. "Liam, Sam?"

"Mac. Chief. Mr. McLane," both agents greeted Mac, his dad, and the present Chief. "We've called the crime unit, but we wanted you to see this first."

Mac's footsteps on the concrete floor were loud. His dad and Daniels were right behind him.

He didn't have to get too close to the freezer to see the body inside. It was frozen and nicely preserved. So, he also didn't have to get close to examine it in order to identify it, either. Although the wonder of how he got folded so nicely in that small compartment did pass through Mac's thoughts.

Before he could speak, Robert let out his own thoughts. "Randy Gresden. I guess he didn't go to Florida or California, after all."

"I'll have to tell Tony he can stop hunting for him," Mac said.

"Unbelievable," Daniels whispered.

Mac thought of Lizzy and looked from Liam to Sam. "Where's Kathleen Gresden now?"

"I don't know," Sam replied. "When she saw she couldn't stop the search of her house by giving us sex, she picked up her keys and left."

Mac met his dad's gaze. "Where would she go?" Then Daniels's words echoed through his thoughts. Kathleen would do whatever was necessary to keep her boys safe from anyone she thought would cause them pain.

"Kathleen Gresden probably blames Lizzy for Stan going to County. I need to get back to the bakery and check on her." And he should have returned her call, too.

Mac's heart already felt as if weights were tied to it, and it was being dragged beneath the surface of a vast, turbulent ocean. In less than two seconds, he had his phone in his hand and he speed dialed her number. Then he knew his heart was drowning when she didn't answer, and the call went to her voice mail.

Chapter Twenty

The quiet was nerve-wracking.

The empty bakery had an eerie feel that caused the hair on Lizzy's arms to stand up.

Lizzy refilled her cup of coffee and sucked in a deep breath. "The last thing I need is to control the customers. I've been alone in here before. This shouldn't bother me."

In the wake of revealing Stan's true Jekyll and Hyde personality, every little noise made her jump.

She speed dialed Mac, but the sweet, female computer voice asking her to leave a message was the answer. "Damn." Next, she dialed Tony. "Are you almost done?" she asked when he answered with a, "Hey..."

She forced her voice to stay light even though it felt far from it.

"Soon. I think. Now that I've found the definite problem with the high school computer network. I wish these damned kids would stop trying to hack around to get past the blocked porn sites. Are you okay?"

"Sure."

"Did you have a big crowd for lunch?"

"Yes, quite a few, but it cleared out a half hour ago. Now, it's really quiet in here, almost too quiet."

"Who was in? Anyone in particular?"

She gave him the idle chit-chat he needed. Obviously, she needed it, too, because it felt good to talk.

She recognized his tactic to keep the conversation easy and mindless. A few of her classmates who had congregated there for brunch to talk about last minute details regarding the reunion were gone now, too. Even the reading area was empty. Some had asked about her cheek. Most others had been polite and said nothing, just pretended it was another day. There had, however, been a great deal of whispering going on in her shop. As if she couldn't hear it. She knew everyone was whispering about her. Or about Stan. Or about her *and*

Stan. She almost felt like she was back walking the halls of the high school.

She didn't care. She ignored it and did her job.

She told him about the mysterious meeting with Chief Daniels. They could only assume the meeting was about Stan. Although why she wouldn't be included, considering she was the one who'd had a knife against her face and now had to wear a stitch in her cheek, she had no idea. Neither did Tony, who promised to be finished shortly.

When she finally hung up, she felt better.

She wished Mac would get back. She wished Tony was back, too. Just how long did it take to fix the high school network problem?

Lizzy drew in a deep breath and relaxed. She was safe. Stan was still in County Lock-Up, where he should be. She picked up a tray of dirty coffee mugs and carried them into the kitchen, needing to stay busy. As she put the tray on the counter next to the dishwasher, she heard the sounds of muffled voices and laughter from out on the walk and she glanced at the clock on the wall. It was time for her usual high school student customers. Where had the afternoon gone?

She started lining the dirty coffee mugs into the dishwasher. Yes, work in her bakery was just what she needed. Maybe now was the time to add in something new, such as a cozy electric fireplace.

The bells over the front door jingled with the arrival of a customer, probably a group of girls needing some caffeine.

"Be right there." she called out from the kitchen as she wondered vaguely why she didn't hear any of the usual girl chatter or laughter and finished with the mugs. She had plenty. She didn't need to take the time now to run the dishwasher.

Her heart skipped when she returned to the main room to find Kathleen Gresden sitting on one of the stools at the counter. "Kathleen?"

Stan's mother was pointedly ignoring her as she read the colorful chalkboard menu that graced the entire wall behind where Lizzy stood. "Hi, Lizzy," she said lightly.

Considering the bright—although probably fake and forced—smile on her lips, one would think she didn't know her son was in jail.

"Hi..."

"I'll have," Kathleen paused, still considering her options. "A pumpkin spice latte and a piece of your famous apple pie. I hear it's the best, even better than my own. But I won't take it personally. Oh, and give me one—no, make it two—of those special twisted donuts you're so known for."

It took a heartbeat or two before Lizzy could get the message to her brain to decipher latte, pie, and donuts. "Okay."

Everything was only a few steps away. A plate, the tray of donuts inside the display case, the pie in the covered cake plate, a mug. Working the bakery was so automatic. She'd served these items countless times. This time, her legs felt as though each one weighed a hundred pounds.

She put the plate of donuts on the counter in front of her soul customer. She used her father's big knife to then cut a piece of pie.

"Oh, cut me an extra big piece," Kathleen said.

Lizzy did and carefully placed the knife on the counter instead of back on the pie plate. Then she slid a clean fork and the plate with a huge slice of pie over the counter next to the donuts. While trying to breathe calmly and appear normal, she made the cup of coffee, never fully turning her back to the counter. She made the coffee an extra great size even though no size had been specified.

She closed her eyes briefly while she envisioned finding it necessary to toss the hot liquid into Kathleen's face in a way to defend herself. She sure as hell hoped it didn't come to that. She hoped she didn't need any defensive action at all, but it was always good to have a plan.

"Mmmm, your pie is delicious, just like Elliot said."

Lizzy watched her chew a big bite before stuffing in a second bite. "What do you want, Kathleen?"

"Now what kind of question is that for a customer?" Kathleen shrugged as if she didn't understand the question. "I'm just here for pie...and donuts...and coffee. Just like all the other customers." She looked around innocently. "Oh, but wait, I think I'm the only one. Business must not be very good today."

Business was just fine, Lizzy bit her tongue to keep from blurting out. And she couldn't for the life of her understand why the place was empty. Usually about this time, her dining area filled up with high school kids as they got off school. And she'd certainly feel better if she wasn't alone with mother of the man who had threatened to cut off her face. She glanced at the door.

Her heart felt like it dropped to her stomach when she saw the *Open* sign was turned to *Closed* and the door was locked. Obviously, the woman across the counter who was woofing down pie had done that. "Kathleen..."

The counter was between them, and Lizzy wanted to keep it that way no matter how much she considered trying to be normal and marching over to turn the sign back.

"I just never took you for being a slut," Kathleen said bluntly.

"What?"

"I mean, you understand...of course, you do. That I would do anything—whatever is necessary—to keep my boys on a straight and narrow and safe path."

Lizzy said nothing. What did *anything necessary* consist of?

"I just never thought you were like some of those other slutty girls."

"I'm not a slut."

Kathleen took a sip of her coffee. And made a face, disgust in her expression. "I really like your pie, but not so much your coffee. It has too much of something, maybe too much cinnamon. I should probably keep to cappuccino. It's hard to tell under all that sugar. I wanted to talk to you about that. You know too much sugar is so bad for Stan. It makes him do..." She paused, rolled her eyes and shook her head, "crazy things. And it interferes with his medication. I'm sure you understand."

Oh, she understood all right. Firsthand, and she had the fingerprints on her throat hidden under another scarf to prove it.

Kathleen grinned. "You know, if there was one thing I learned from my husband, it was that men are unpredictable. Wouldn't you agree?" She stuffed another big bite of pie into her mouth and chewed. Once she swallowed, she droned on, sounding as if she might be trying to lecture her little kids in class. "I really didn't get angry, and it didn't bother me at all that Stan likes your pie better than mine. Especially when I noticed he was spending a lot of time here with you. First, it was just skipping breakfast. Then, it was not needing a lunch made. After that, he started being late for supper. Obviously, he was feeling something for you. It's been a long time since he showed interest in another woman. I mean Kelly Mattis really sent him for a loop, screwing everyone in town, trying to extort money from him because he had a little difficulty, you know—getting it up. I mean what man doesn't? Now that I think about it, Randy never had difficulty." She chuckled bitterly.

The sound of it sent a shiver up Lizzy's back.

"Hell, that bastard could hit me once and be ready to fuck one of the horses in Stapleton's pasture. That, of course, is old news. Back to Stan. After Kelly got what she deserved, there was that girl at college that he kept seeing. Not that he took any classes there. No, he lied to me and told me he needed to visit your brother. As it happened, she was just another slut who didn't understand my boy. And again, his mommy had to step in and fix things."

She took a large drink of coffee. Then kind of stuck out her tongue. "Yep, no more of that nasty stuff. Can I get a cappuccino?"

Lizzy ignored the request and stared at her customer.

Kathleen sighed and continued as though there'd been no interruption. "Do you have any idea how tired I am? All I ever do is work to fix things. I mean, I feel like I spent the boys' entire childhoods on the phone with either a principal or a teacher. 'Elliot pushed another child off the slide. Stan isn't doing his homework, and his leaf collection is two days late.'" She spoke in a mocking voice, imitating a teacher. "Hell, I didn't even know he needed a leaf collection then."

She let out a loud huff. Her voice was so calm; she could have been discussing the beautiful fall weather. "Anyway, getting back to now. After that slut was out of the picture, I was afraid Stan would never be interested in another woman again."

Lizzy said nothing, just stared, terror filling her to the point she couldn't breathe, her guard up so high the hair on the back of her neck was standing. Pieces began to fall into place, horrid, frightening pieces. Where the hell was Mac when she needed him? Her phone played a familiar tune, indicating an incoming call.

"Don't even think about answering that," Kathleen said lightly. Once the song of Lizzy's phone stopped, she went on, "I suppose something in your apple pie struck Stan's heart. And I thought okay, *Lizzy comes from a better family. Maybe she'll be good enough for my boy.* Then, like all the others, you failed to understand him. It's a shame, too, because I really like you, Lizzy. And you have made this place into the most wonderful, inviting bakery-slash-coffee shop. Everyone loves coming in here, including me."

Thoughts of how to escape were flashing through Lizzy's mind. There was the back door, but it required a key to open the deadbolt. Would she be quick enough to get it open?

There was the front door. Could she get around the counter and to the door fast enough? What about the front windows? Dare she attempt crashing through?

There were the stairs leading up to her apartment, but her sliding barn door was locked and also required a key because Lizzy was always afraid someone might venture up there unnoticed if she didn't.

She needed time.

She needed to outfox an evident fox, someone cunning with the obvious ability to kill and get away with it for a decade. Working to keep her hands from shaking, she grabbed a clean mug before filling it with coffee.

"What are you doing?" Kathleen asked.

"Just allowing myself a cup of coffee. I always treat myself after a day working in the bakery."

Again, Kathleen read over the wall-covered chalkboard menu. "What's your favorite flavor?"

"I like to keep things simple. My favorite is a coffee just called Donut Shop."

"Oh, how funny," Kathleen said, although there wasn't an ounce of laughter in her voice.

"So...Kelly was trying to get money from Stan?" Now that was something she'd never heard about. It was no secret, however, that Kelly seemed to want to sample every guy around.

"A hundred dollars. She said he had to give her a hundred dollars, or she was going to tell everyone at school how he couldn't...you know. Then she happened to see him, just like you apparently did. He had something—I don't remember now what it was—maybe one of the neighbor's puppies in our garage. And her price went to five hundred. I found him crying like a little baby, and he told me everything. I told him to tell Kelly—in person, no texting, no phone, no record—to meet him after the dance in the tunnel. I knew no one would go there. I didn't even figure she'd be found for a while, considering the fact no one ever had the guts to go in there. I guess the idea of being given five hundred dollars kept any fear of the place at bay for her. She marched right in, wearing the ugliest, stupid high heels I've ever seen. I'd been hiding in the tunnel in the dark for two hours. I was cold and tired and hungry. I saw her drive up with Daniels. The way his car was shaking, I knew she was giving him a good time. I even considered sneaking closer, taking a picture of the two of them with my phone, and giving her a taste of her own blackmail medicine. Considering how she was obviously doing everyone in pants, I figured it probably wouldn't be enough to stop her. I also figured she wouldn't stop after five hundred—even if I did have it to give to her, which I didn't. Frank...Chief Daniels—of course, he wasn't Chief back then—sat in his car for the longest time, even after she was dead. And I always had the impression he didn't know she even headed into the tunnel. I finally got tired of waiting for him to leave, and I decided to go out the other end, which would have been a longer trek home, but who cared? And there was a pickup truck parked out there." She grinned an evil grin. "I didn't even know it was you and Chief McLane's boy until later. Luckily, when I ran the other way, out the other tunnel entrance, Frank was gone."

Lizzy put the cup of coffee on the counter so she didn't spill it on herself, given the fact she could no longer keep herself from shaking. She didn't, however, let go of the handle. Aside from words and the pie knife a few feet away, it was the only apparent weapon within reach.

Other puzzle pieces were falling into place for Lizzy. "You were in the hospital after that for a day or two."

"Oh, yeah, I almost forgot that part. Randy broke three of my ribs. Usually, he was so careful to keep things hidden, to hit me so no one else would know. This time, he managed to puncture a lung." Kathleen glanced up as if she could see the memory on the ceiling. "Chief McLane wanted me to press charges. He visited me in the hospital and told me with the hospital records, and the fact I had two sons at home, he could probably put Randy away for a year."

"But you didn't." Lizzy remembered.

"You're damned right I didn't. Randy was like a slippery snake. He would never have gone to jail, not for more than a day or maybe a week at most. He would have managed to slither out from under any charges. He probably would have killed me. In the end, it didn't matter. He decided to disappear on his own. I got out of the hospital only to come home and find he'd packed up and left with nothing more than a stupid note that said he was sorry for all the pain and he thought it was best he left before he did anything worse. I figured Chief McLane must have said something that finally got through to him. I don't think I slept for weeks, worrying that if I did, I'd wake up to find him sitting at the kitchen table, demanding to know where his pancakes were. Then I worried about what to do with the shop, but Stan was a natural there. He always had been. It was the one good thing Stan's father had done for him—teaching him that trade. Stan was always good with machines. The poor kid could hardly write a decent paragraph, but he could make jewelry in shops class. I even tried to send the cops into a direction of the boys in high school as being Kelly's killer by putting a bracelet on her. I knew all the shops classes made the same bracelet. Stan had given me one and told me not to feel bad if any other moms were wearing the same thing. I never heard of anything coming of that evidence. Maybe one of the many she'd screwed had already given her a bracelet."

She paused and took a deep breath. "Oh, but Stan, my creative boy. He could make a great bookshelf in woodworking. And he could detail a car or fix a dent better than his father, which was also good, since a few days later he hurt his knee at football practice and his scholarship was lost." She smiled the first genuine, although small, smile since coming in. "That was like a knife to my heart even though Stan didn't seem to mind. In fact, he embraced working in the shop after school, helped put food on the table while I got my teaching degree, and has told me many times he has no regrets about taking over his father's shop."

Lizzy's insides felt like an earthquake was happening in her soul. After everything she'd just heard, it registered at least a nine point five on the Richter scale. She forced in an even breath, mentally patting herself on the back with the idea she was keeping the terror swirling through her well-hidden.

The sense that Kathleen was approaching the end of her story heightened her fight or flight mode. She was going to have to do something. She knew full well Kathleen was not about to smile and thank her for the coffee, pie, donuts and nice chat, and then mosey on out the door. Not after *that* story.

In fact, if she didn't think she was about to have to fight for her life, she'd compliment Kathleen. It was a truly amazing story in itself. The fact that the woman had managed to keep it a secret all this time made it even more astonishing.

She wasn't given much time to dwell on it, though, because like a snake striking, Kathleen grabbed the pie knife before Lizzy could.

In almost the same instant, Lizzy tossed the hot mug of coffee in her face.

Kathleen screamed but managed to keep the knife in her hand as she slid off the stool, her face dripping and coffee staining her shirt.

Heart racing, Lizzy wasted no time. She sprinted around the counter to the front door. It was her best option. The front of the building was all glass. She hoped someone would see her struggle and come to help. Also, not that she liked the idea any more than before, but she was prepared to jump through one of the front windows to escape. It was the one on her left where there was one fake wedding cake that became her target. But she didn't make it.

She was shorter, her stride smaller than that of Kathleen, who stood taller and had longer legs. Which was why Lizzy had mistaken her for a man in the dark at the entrance to Marston's Tunnel. Kathleen tackled her, obviously taking lessons from her son's high school football days.

Her back to the floor, Lizzy fought, keeping her hands and feet kicking, striking, holding wherever possible. She also fought to stay focused. There was a flash as the knife sliced through the air and then a burst of white-hot pain as Kathleen managed to cut her arm with the pie knife.

Lizzy didn't exert the energy to scream, just breathed and worked to focus on the fight, grabbing Kathleen's wrist that wielded the blade. She was at a disadvantage having Kathleen's weight on top of her.

"Target points," Lizzy said out loud, trying to remember. It was another amazing moment. Everything was happening fast, but felt like slow motion. Everything was clear. She heard her own breaths, felt her heart racing in her chest, and knew she could not stop fighting or it would mean her life as Kathleen held the knife raised above her.

She was not going to die by her own father's pie knife.

She was not.

With the sound of her own words, she remembered the target points. Keeping her elbow locked holding the knife at bay with her grip on Kathleen's wrist, she attacked with her other hand with three quick sequenced blows. One to Kathleen's left breast, one to her solar plexus, and the third to the throat.

Bam, bam, bam.

None of the three were enough to cause lasting damage, but they—especially the one to the throat—gave Lizzy what she needed.

Time and distraction as Kathleen gasped and struggled for a breath.

This, in turn, gave Lizzy control of the hand that held the knife. She let it arc down in the direction it was pointed. Only she took it further, holding tight and directing it until the blade sank right into Kathleen's midsection. The shock on her face was time-stopping.

And for what felt like a life time, the two of them hung there, suspended, Kathleen straddling Lizzy, who still grasped Kathleen's wrist.

Lizzy was terrified to let go. Her breaths were loud in the silence. Her opponent, however, appeared to have stopped breathing as she stared down at the knife handle protruding from her belly.

It wasn't a lifetime. It wasn't even a few seconds. Blood began to pour from Kathleen's wound. She opened her mouth as if she tried to speak but uttered no words. Maybe it was from the punch to her throat, maybe it was from the shock of having a knife in her gut.

Lizzy scrambled to escape the seeping blood. Her action sent the taller woman tumbling away. She used her feet to slide backside across the wood polished floor to put some distance between them. The moment was horrific. All she could do was stare as more of Kathleen's blood soaked her bakery floor. A strange, absurd thought of Kelly dying in the same manner, and what goes around comes around whirled through her mind.

Then the door crashed in, sounding like an explosion in the silence. There was Chief Daniels, Mac's dad, two men in suits whom Lizzy didn't recognize. And Mac.

She'd never been so glad to see him.

Mac's hands were on her arms, hauling her to her feet. His mouth was moving, too, but she couldn't seem to hear any words over the rushing of blood and the roaring sound in her ears. There was blood on her shirt. Then she remembered Kathleen had cut her arm with the knife. Strange how it didn't hurt anymore.

She felt so dizzy. Her knees were so weak, all she wanted to do was lean against Mac's chest. She breathed in his enticing, inviting scent to get the coppery burning smell of blood out of her nose. Oh, his embrace, there was no safer place. She just needed to rest for a few minutes, and then she'd tell him everything Kathleen had said. She closed her eyes and listened the to the strong beat of his heart.

Chapter Twenty-One

Mac breathed and worked to ignore the pain that felt like a coiled snake in his leg as he waited for the guard to buzz him into the interior of the county jail. The barred door automatically closed behind him with a loud sound of mechanism and lock and finality. Three locked entrances later, he found himself seated before a small glass partitioned booth. Sitting didn't ease the pain in the wound in his leg. Stan Gresden sat on the other side.

Stan stared at him for a long moment, an unnerving grin on his face. Then he picked up the corded handset of the nearby telephone. Mac did the same.

"You shouldn't have bothered to waste your time coming down here, Mac. My lawyer's going to get me out of here probably within the hour. You could have just talked to me back in Mossy Point. Hell, you could have come to my shop or met me at the Streetside, and we could have downed a few together."

Mac shrugged. "Okay, but in case you haven't heard, your mother tried to kill Lizzy earlier this afternoon. Before that, she confessed to killing Kelly Mattis, and to killing the girl you liked to visit at Mizzou named Sara Gibson."

Mac let that information get digested, and it didn't settle well. In fact, Stan bit his bottom lip. Defeat was etched in his expression for the first time. "Sara?" Stan stared at the table in front of him, unable to meet Mac's gaze.

"That's right. And your mom got stabbed. She's still in surgery."

"Is she going to be all right?"

"She's expected to be. Of course, she'll wake up handcuffed to the bed."

"I need to get out of here." Now he sounded like a desperate man. "I need to take care of Elliot."

It tore at Mac to see him. Stan was his friend, his expert receiver who had surely been dealt a horribly bad hand. Mac let out a long, heavy breath. "Elliot's fine. Tell me about your father."

Puzzled confusion crossed Stan's expression, but was quickly gone. "I haven't heard from him. I always figured he was in Florida like his note said."

"He's been frozen in a freezer in your mom's storage unit for a long time, perfectly preserved, still has a little frozen blood in his mullet and a knot on his head. And your mom spilled a lot a few hours ago. A hell of a lot. Despite all her confession, she didn't know anything about your dad. As a matter of fact, she was in the hospital the night he supposedly skipped town and made his way into the tundra. Would you like to tell me about it...while you have the opportunity?"

"I don't think I want to tell you anything."

"It's only reasonable to tell you Chief Daniel's is preparing to arrest Elliot. After all, if you didn't kill him and put him in the freezer, and your mom couldn't because she was in a hospital bed, Elliot's the only evident suspect. I would imagine, given his simple way of thinking, he'll probably tell us what he knows. I doubt he'll fare very well in prison. He's too nice, too trusting."

Dark, red fury filled Stan's features. Mac wondered if this was how he looked when he was strangling Lizzy. "You leave Elliot out of this!" His words were spoken through gritted teeth. "And you get me the hell out of here so I can take care of him."

"I don't think that's going to happen. If you talk to me, maybe I can keep him from being arrested. Right now, he's in the tender care of the Mansford Home. You know, the place for those with mental challenges. It's a nice place, and I think he'll like it...a lot better than prison."

Again, it tore at Mac. He didn't want to threaten Elliot, and it left a bitter taste in his mouth and seemed to set a fire in his leg wound. He had no intention of allowing Elliot to go to prison. He needed answers. He was exhausted and wanted nothing more than to get back to Lizzy.

He figured it was his turn to get a massage. Still, he was very certain, she was going to need something to help her sleep after the day she'd had.

Stan met his gaze evenly, but sounded more defeated than ever. "Off the record?"

"Off the record," Mac agreed. Right then, he was ready to take it however he could get it.

"My father was a prick. There was never any secret in that. He broke my mom's ribs just because she made baked potatoes instead of mashed. He hit her and knocked her down, then kicked her until she couldn't breathe. Do you have any idea what it's like to watch that? Because I watched it my whole life."

Mac had no idea how that must have felt. He pursed his lips and took a deep breath, blinking back tears that filled his eyes. His best friend didn't deserve this. No one deserved this. He always felt he did everything he could for Stan. Now he was left wondering what more he should have done. Or could have done. He swallowed down a huge lump in his throat and let his friend go on.

"Life with my old man was this vicious cycle of getting drunk, getting mad, needing to lash out and hurt someone, feeling sorry, feeling guilty, needing a drink to wash down the guilt, then getting drunk again. Sometimes, if we were lucky enough, he'd get drunk and pass out before he got mad enough to hurt someone. I guess after he put my mom in the hospital, he was feeling exceptionally guilty because when Elliot and I got home from school, I saw he'd been drinking the hard shit."

For a moment, Mac wasn't even sure he could sit still to hear the rest of the story. He stared at Stan through the glass partition, wondering just how different his friend's life would have been had he had a different parent. But then, kids never got to choose their parents.

Stan continued. "And he was pretty drunk by the time Elliot and I walked in the door. I was tired. I had had Elliot sit on the bleachers while we had football practice. I never let him go home alone anyway.

I sure didn't let him be alone with Dad when I knew mom wouldn't be there. Anyway, we found him drunk and mean and demanding supper as if he forgot my mom was in the hospital because he put her there. He broke dishes and yelled and cussed and drooled spit like some rabid animal. Before I could stop him, he knocked me right off my feet. Then stomped on my leg. *He* ended my football career. *He* took my scholarship from me. I made it like it happened at practice the next night. And I shuffled around in agony all the next day before that practice so no one knew. Getting back to my dad—when he was going to stomp on my leg again, Elliot rammed into him. I remember Elliot was crying."

He paused and gave a small, sad smile. "You know how he is. He's either happy or sad. I yelled for him to stop. I was afraid Dad would hurt him. I have to say, my dad was a prick in every way. He'd hit me. He'd hit my mom. He was pretty careful when it came to Elliot. And, at that moment, given Dad was worse than I'd ever seen him, I was certain he would hurt my challenged brother. So, I screamed for Elliot to stop and go to his room, away from me and our old man, told him to lock himself in and hide under his bed."

Stan paused in his explanation and chuckled bitterly. "He didn't. He tackled Dad better than anyone on the team could have. He took him right off his feet and sent him tumbling down the basement steps."

Stan took a deep breath that sounded a little like relief at finally getting the horror of that moment off his shoulders. "I was just glad to see Elliot didn't go with him. The sounds of him going down the stairs and landing on the floor—*thump, thump, thump, plop*—still haunt my nights. There was no rail, as you well know, and he didn't go all the way down via the steps. He fell over the side and hit the concrete floor."

He paused as if he had to re-digest the memory. "I told Elliot he was just sleeping, passed out like he usually was. I knew, the moment I managed to get down there, he was dead. I was terrified no one would believe me if I told them what happened. I was even more terrified they would believe me, and Elliot would go to jail. Either way, I didn't trust in telling. I know your father tried to stop my dad at every opportunity, but he always found a way to slither out from under the law—which I might add never seemed to be on our side. So, I wrote the note that sounded so much like his guilty side it really could have been like he wrote it. After Elliot went to sleep, I dragged him to his own truck and put him in the back. It was the biggest workout I've ever had, especially since it felt like my leg was on fire. I didn't really know what to do with him, so I took him to the storage unit, plugged in the old freezer that was there, and was glad when I saw it still worked. He used to use it in his hunting days to store pelts and animals before having them processed." Stan grinned. "I suppose I should always be thankful he gave up his hunting and his guns before he started drinking and punching."

Mac swallowed down the bile that burned his throat. He had no idea how much Stan had had to carry around.

"I shoved his truck over the ledge up at the strip mine lake. It sank pretty quickly, and we've never had a drought dry enough to reveal it because he couldn't leave if his truck was still here. I really didn't plan to leave him there in the freezer, and later I thought I should have sent him into the lake with his truck. That way, if it was discovered, everyone would think he drove over the ledge while he was drunk. God knows it was probably eighty proof running through his veins that night. But then, I guess I didn't actually *plan* any of it, but it seemed to work out. No one found the truck and no one thought about the freezer. Everyone seemed to believe the story written in the note about him moving away to keep his family safe and about being sorry for all the years of pain. And, as days melted into weeks and then months, I kind of gave up on ever moving him. My mom only griped once about the price of the storage unit going up, but she didn't connect it to the fact that the electricity was now being used. If she ever opened the freezer and found him, she didn't say anything about it."

"It was an accident," Mac pointed out. His throat was dry, the words were painful.

Stan chuckled bitterly. "Yeah. My whole life with him was an accident. And I eased the pain of by sniffing some of the chemicals at the shop." He shrugged as if the idea of that was no big deal.

They were quiet for a long moment. Then Stan's features softened. "I'm sorry about Lizzy. She's a nice woman. I never meant to hurt her. No one ever saw me like that before. And I...did a little snorting before that. I don't even remember most of what happened after she walked in."

"I know."

"Will you tell her for me?"

"Yes."

"I always wondered if my mother had something to do with Kelly Mattis. I never asked. I guess I was too afraid to know for certain."

"I'll bet," Mac said. He figured Stan as a teenager was probably keeping enough secrets with his dad's death.

Again, there was silence over the intercom for a long moment. Then Stan asked, "Anything else you want to ask me about?"

Mac shrugged then shook his head. "I think that pretty well covers everything." He knew it was going to take a while to digest it all. How Stan finished out his senior year carrying the weight of this and still making the grade, he had no idea. He had, after all, had trouble seeing the year through with the memory of a blood-covered Kelly Mattis haunting his dreams, and considering how things worked out—or didn't work out—with Lizzy. He didn't think he could have functioned with something as heavy as a death like that of Randy Gresden on his back, even if it was an accident.

Stan nodded. Mac took the receiver away from his ear. Stan's, "Mac?" stopped him from hanging up.

"Yeah?" At least his throat was no longer burning.

"Take good care of Lizzy. The two of you deserve some happiness together after all this time."

Mac nodded.

He couldn't agree more.

He didn't remember the drive back to Mossy Point. He barely acknowledged Tony, who unlocked and opened the door of the bakery and let him in. His steps across the floor sounded loud and heavy and echoed in the stillness. He was pretty sure someone had branded his leg with a hot iron. Then he was in Lizzy's arms. Where he belonged.

****

Sweet heavens, the last time Lizzy saw Mac like this, he stood in the middle of the police station and her father had just told him to never speak to her or approach her in any way.

Defeated.

Beaten.

Hurting.

Just seeing so much pain etched into his strong features made her feel like long, ghostly fingers had slithered into her chest and tried to rip her heart out through her throat.

Whatever he'd just learned, or heard or done, it surpassed her own horrid day. She didn't hesitate, but ignored her brother, rushed to the man who held her heart, and took him in her arms.

He crumpled into her embrace like a child needing comfort, and Lizzy gave him everything she had as she held him close, wishing she could soothe all his pain.

"Tell me what happened," she said softly.

Against her shoulder, he shook his head. "Not yet. I can't yet."

"Okay." She settled for just holding him.

Over his shoulder, she met Tony's gaze, who whispered softly, "I'll lock the door on my way out."

She nodded.

Once outside, Tony used his key to lock the newly fixed deadbolt. He waved through the window, blew her a kiss and mouthed, "I'll call you later." Then he was gone.

She didn't know what exactly Mac needed. She knew they needed each other. Desperately. She let him go just enough to lead him up the stairs to her apartment.

"I keep telling myself maybe none of this would have happened if I hadn't come back." Mac's words were tight and harsh.

"All of this was happening with you not being here. It just chose this week to come to light. I don't think it would have made any difference if you were here or not. I'm just glad you are, so you can hold me."

With her hand tucked in his, she led him to her bed and eased him onto it. He lay back on his back and covered his eyes with his arm as if, perhaps if he didn't look, all the horror of the past few days might disappear. She understood how he felt. She'd wished she could close her eyes to it, too. It didn't work. When she closed her eyes, she still saw Kathleen with a knife over her. Or Stan's eyes bloodshot bulging as he choked her. If anyone had told her six months ago that these two people she'd trusted would have done a one-eighty and tried to kill her this week, she would have laughed it off and never believed it.

With little hesitation, she climbed on him and straddled his legs. "Does this hurt your leg with me sitting on you like this?"

"No."

Slowly, carefully, she unbuttoned the buttons of his shirt.

"What are you doing?" He asked without opening his eyes.

"Making you more comfortable. You helped me through something horrid with a wonderful massage. I thought I'd do the same for you." She hoped for something more. Ever since he'd made love to her, she'd thought of little else. Even with the threats on her life, making love with Mac was always on the back burner. After only one time, she knew without a doubt there was no better place to be than in his arms with him tucked deep inside her, connecting to her as no one else had. Ever.

With her fingers spread, she massaged her palms down his chest to his abdomen. His skin was tanned, a rich color of honey. Perfect, flawless, not quite a six-pack, but hard, well-muscled, except for...

"You've got another scar here."

"Yeah." He covered her hands with his as his gaze caught hers and held it hostage. "Ignore it, please. Keep touching me."

"I plan to."

"Good."

"I was on your lap straddling you like this after the dance when we were in your truck. Do you remember?"

"Yes."

"Me, too," she admitted. She kept one palm flat against his skin as she worked his belt and his fly with her other. When he helped her, she shifted slightly to allow him to wiggle out of his jeans. "Have I told you how much your boxer briefs turn me on?"

"No."

"They do."

"Good."

"The blue ones are sexy, but red is my favorite color."

"I'll wear red for you tomorrow."

"I can't wait." There was something about sitting on top of him that made her feel bold and sexy. She found herself drawn to the sense of control. "For now, you should take these off."

"In a minute." He wasn't as slow or determined as she had been with his shirt as he made quick work of removing the sweater she'd put on after returning from the Emergency Room where she'd gone with her arm bleeding. She took her hands off him just long enough to raise her arms so he could slide the sweater over her head.

"How's your arm?" He gave the brown bandage on her arm a glance before he placed his hands on her breasts through the lace of the bra she wore.

"It's still a little numb from the shot they gave me before they put in the stitches, but it's fine. I took a pain pill, too. Better living through chemistry." She drew in a breath, relishing in the wonderful, erotic touch of his fingers on her nipples. It was enough to send a delicious shiver up her back.

"Cold?" he asked.

"I was when I got home. I drank two cups of hot tea trying to warm up. Now that I'm with you, I feel fine. Your hands feel so good. They fill me with warmth that makes me shiver."

"Are you sleepy?"

"Not at all. You?"

"After listening to Stan, I felt like I'd been beaten and I could sleep for days, but not anymore." As he spoke, he caressed the back of her shoulders before he unhooked her bra. The garment fell to the floor beside the bed, sounding like a whispered sigh.

And his hands were on her. Skin to skin. His warmth melted into her, starting tiny fires in her soul as he explored every inch of her breasts with his palms and fingertips.

"Do you have any idea how much I want you?" he asked.

She grinned down at the bulge in his blue boxer briefs. "I have a pretty good idea." She climbed away from him for a moment, just long enough to kick off her shoes and scramble out of her jeans. He devoured her with his gaze as she seductively peeled off her clothes and kept his hand on her, as if he was afraid if he let her go, she might disappear. He stayed on his back on her bed and wiggled out of his boxer briefs when she was about to climb back on.

Suddenly, he stopped. "Hell..."

"What?"

"You know, the last time we didn't use any protection. I meant to stop at the drug store and get something, and given all the excitement, I just never got the chance."

She had thought about that two seconds after he was inside her as he'd had her held up against the wall. Had that only been a few days ago? It felt like a lifetime. She caressed his lips with her fingertips. "It's okay. I like you in me with nothing."

He chuckled. "Like you know it any other way."

She chuckled too, but then grew serious. "And having your baby would be the greatest gift to me. But to ease your mind I know we aren't in the danger zone when it comes to my cycle. We should be safe."

"You're sure?"

"I've always been like clockwork. So, yes. Would you please stop making me wait? I've needed you all afternoon. Even when I was getting my arm stitched up, what got me through it was knowing you'd soon be holding me and living up to the promise you made of making love to me again." She took the initiative, leaned up, shifted her hips, and slipped onto him.

His groan was music to her ears.

She thought he'd lie there and let her do what she wanted, but he sat up. A moment later, they were both sitting, facing one another. She was tucked in the pocket of his lap, his legs under her, as she held him with her legs around him the same way, belly to belly, her breasts tight against his chest. And the two of them lost within one another.

Wonderful, was all she could think. Just plain perfect and wonderful. She knew he had a job that called him, and maybe soon it would take him away from her.

For now, they held each other so close she didn't know where she ended and he began. For now, they were joined as she'd never been to another person.

She held on tight as he kissed her again and again, each touch of his lips adding fuel to the fire he set in her.

And she enjoyed every moment of the ride.

Chapter Twenty-Two

Friday

In Lizzy's arms, finally given the night to explore every aspect of her, to know her as he'd never known anyone else, Mac was given a new beginning. Another chance, one he was all ready to take. He slept with her tucked against him. He woke several times through the night, once to find her sleeping with his chest as her pillow. A second time, he woke to find her soft backside against the front of him. He held her closer to him. In her sleep, she molded perfectly to him.

He woke to the morning light to find her awake and smiling at him.

And he determined the only thing better than sleeping with her in his arms was having her there waking up next to him.

"Good morning." Her voice was husky with sleep.

"Good morning." He kissed her. "Do you know how delicious you are in the morning?"

"I doubt that."

"Don't."

She started to slide out of bed.

"Where are you going?"

"I'm heading downstairs to start the coffee."

"Don't open today. Stay in bed all day with me. You need your rest. We need to rest together."

She grinned. "I'm sure the town will be buzzing after what happened yesterday. I need to be open. And I feel fine. Take your time getting up. I'll be downstairs, and maybe we can sneak up here later for a quickie." She kissed him and slipped away before he could stop her.

"I'll hold you to that," he said, but she was already closing the bathroom door.

The rich smell of coffee and the thought of her great apple pie led him downstairs a short time later. He heard the soft music of the radio playing over the speakers Lizzy had. Yes, he could do this every day for the rest of his life—sleep with her, make love to her all night, wake up with her in his arms, and kiss her good morning. Then he could join her for coffee as she started her bakery day.

He wanted this routine, and he planned to work things out so he could have it.

He stepped downstairs to find her father sitting on a stool at the counter, appearing to be waiting for him.

Mac paused and assessed the situation, just as he always did when it came to his job. Even though this concerned Lizzy, which was about as far from a 'job' as life could ever get for Mac.

He could turn left and just shuttle out the door of the bakery. After all, his truck was parked right outside. He could see it through the front windows. The window of the front door was intact, and the lock was new. The part of the door jamb that he'd busted yesterday in order to get in to save Lizzy had already been fixed thanks to Tony, but needed some paint.

Mac didn't turn left. With purpose—despite the way his stomach seemed to sink with each step—he made his way to the counter and sat down on the empty stool next to Luca Signorino. There was an empty mug and a pot of coffee on the counter within arm's reach. Yes, Lizzy's father was definitely waiting for him. And expecting him.

Luca filled the mug with steaming coffee before sliding it over the counter to him.

From the kitchen Mac heard the mumbled voices of Lizzy, Tony, and their mother, Valentina.

"Good morning," Luca greeted him quietly while he carefully sipped his coffee. He watched his family through the kitchen door and didn't yet look at Mac.

Mac had to clear his throat before he could speak. "Good morning."

For a long moment, both men were quiet. Mac waited and took a sip of the strong, hot coffee Luca had poured for him, careful not to drink too much and burn his throat. He did his best to appear casual, but felt far from it. "Did you just get here?"

"Val and I took the red eye. Tony picked us up at the airport."

"I see."

Finally, Luca turned and met his gaze evenly. "I doubt you see it all."

Mac more or less doubted that, too, but had the feeling by the time this conversation was over, his eyes would be opened.

"We had to come and check on our children, make certain Lizzy was all right."

"Of course," Mac agreed. He wouldn't have expected anything less.

"We also wanted to give Lizzy a new pie cutting knife. I understand the other was taken as evidence."

"Yes." He was actually surprised the bakery wasn't sealed off, but there were very few—if any— questions left unanswered this morning.

"I'm also here because I have a confession to make."

Mac did his best not to appear surprised. "Oh?"

"I never expected you to live up to my instructions I gave that night so long ago when I picked my daughter up at the police station, when I told you to stay away from her. I was certain I'd catch her sneaking out to meet you, or I'd hear about the two of you being somewhere or doing something together." He took a deep breath. "However, you proved to be a very honorable young man and followed my rule."

Mac had to clear his voice before he could speak. "Yes."

"I was wrong in making that rule. My daughter was miserable for a long time. As I think you may have been as well, correct?"

"Yes, sir."

The older man nodded. "I am sorry for that."

Mac had to swallow past the lump in his throat. This was the last thing he'd expected. "Apology accepted."

"I thought she would get over you. I thought you would both move on. And perhaps she did. At least until you stepped back in here. Now,

I admit I am glad she did not. And also, that you did not. Thank you for saving her."

"Oh, I think she saved herself. I pretty much busted in the door after the fireworks were over." He did his best to forget the sight of Lizzy on the floor and Kathleen on top of her that he glimpsed through the window as he raced to reach the door. There had been so much blood, at first it was all he'd been able to focus on. And he hadn't had any idea from where it had all come. At least at first.

"No, if you hadn't returned earlier this week, things might be different. Lizzy might still be trying to give her heart to a man who might hurt her, or a man whose mother would probably eventually hurt her. Or worse. I'm certain you saved my daughter in more ways than I can count, and I thank you."

"You're welcome." He almost said it was his job. After all, saving Lizzy from everything from possibly breaking a nail when she opened a car door to a robber stepping into her bakery was now his main job as far as he was concerned. And it had nothing to do with the badge or gun he carried.

"And while I feel you have become a very honorable man, I must ask your intentions." Luca let his gaze stray to the stairs that led up to Lizzy's apartment and he left the rest of the question unspoken—*now that you've obviously slept with my daughter.*

Mac asked his own question in reply. "May I have your permission to ask her to marry me, sir?"

For several antagonizing heartbeats, Luca watched his family in the kitchen and remained silent. And Mac waited, holding his breath, thinking his—hopefully—future father-in-law was prolonging giving an answer just to torture him.

Finally, Luca met his gaze, setting his coffee mug down on the counter with a thud that sounded loud in the empty bakery. "Permission granted, son."

Mac smiled, holding back the whoop of excitement that threatened to bubble out of him. Then a great sense of pride washed over him at the idea of Luca calling him son, just like his own dad called him. "Thank you."

Luca gave him an easy smile and offered his hand.

Mac took it and shook it.

"We can turn the closed sign around now and let the customers in."

Mac blinked and it dawned on him that Luca had been waiting to open until after he talked to him. Lizzy stood in the kitchen doorway, wiping her hands on a towel, the smile on her face warm and beautiful, the white apron she wore sprinkled with white powder that could have been powdered sugar or flour. Mac smiled back.

Luca slipped off the stool. At the front door, he flipped over the sign before he opened it to welcome a few customers who waited out on the front walk.

Mac wasn't really surprised to see the customers were Tiffany and Dane Kizer, both of whom greeted him then hugged Lizzy before paying respects to her parents.

"Come in! Welcome," Luca greeted them. "Today we are celebrating. Everyone eats pie and gets coffee on the house! And—" he put an arm around Tiffany, "I suppose before I head back to Florida, you, your husband, Tony, and I should sit down and have a talk."

For a moment the entire room was so still, Mac was certain no one even breathed.

Tiffany stared up at Luca with wide eyes.

"Don't be so surprised, Tiffany," Luca said, his voice softening. "While Val and I are traditional, we are neither blind nor stupid, nor closed-hearted when it comes to our children. So don't try and keep any more secrets from us." He lightly kissed her cheek before letting her go.

Mac noticed Tony was blinking away tears.

Luca opened the front door again and greeted Mac's mom and dad. Robert shook Luca's hand with enthusiasm. "It's nice to see you." After greeting Luca and Valentina, Ginna hugged Mac. His dad squeezed his arm before giving Lizzy a quick hug.

"We're so glad you're all right," Ginna said when she hugged Lizzy.

A moment later, Mac's brother, Gabe and his very pregnant wife, Suzanne, caused the bells over the door to jingle with their entrance. Gabe gave Mac a brotherly punch to his shoulder before hugging him close.

This was turning into a regular party.

Luca met Mac's gaze. "And *you* have a question for my daughter. Get on with it."

Lizzy stepped close to him.

"Did you know they were here?" he whispered.

"That's your question?" she asked with a chuckle.

"Just the first one."

"I came down to find them here and couldn't sneak back up to warn you. Sorry. I should have checked my phone. At least then I would have then seen Tony's warning texts."

Luca placed a fatherly hand on Mac's shoulder. "Don't make me change my honorable opinion of you."

Mac gave a slight shake of his head and bit his lip to keep from hooting with laughter. This was like sweet, white icing on the horrible cake of the week.

He took both of Lizzy's hands in his. Then, considering her father watched and his parents were there, he thought he'd better do this right. He dropped to one knee before her.

The surprise on her face was beautiful and priceless.

"Maybe we should be doing this outside of Marston's Tunnel," he muttered.

Behind him, her father said. "No."

She grinned down at him, and then bit her lip as if she might burst out laughing.

He grew serious. "I don't have a ring to give you—at least not yet. And while we need to slow things down a little, I want nothing more than to take things day by day with you. My job is up in the air right now, so I'm not really sure what I'll be doing in the future, but Elizabeth Signorino, whatever it is, I want to be doing it with you beside me."

"That sounds like a plan to me." Lizzy's voice was filled with happiness.

He stood up. Then she was in his arms, and he was vaguely aware of those he loved around them applauding.

"What kind of a proposal was that?" her father asked.

"A perfect one, Dad." Lizzy snuggled deeper into his embrace.

Luca was perplexed and gave a slight shake of his head. "Young people these days," he muttered. "We are doomed."

In Mac's arms, Lizzy laughed.

Mac was home, surrounded by family and the inviting aroma of pastry and coffee. Lizzy was in his arms, safe. His damned leg didn't hurt at all. He felt the cloud that had hung over his hometown was beginning to fade.

It was, indeed, perfect.

Turn the page to enjoy more of Lizzy and Mac's story in an excerpt from SMALL TOWN STORM, the next in the series. Reminder: all books by Allie Harrison are stand-alone stories.

SMALL TOWN STORM

Prologue

Tuesday

"Nine-one-one, what's your emergency?"

"Please help. I think I'm having a stroke. Or maybe a heart attack."

"Ma'am? What are your symptoms? Where are you?"

"I'm at home. I...Please. Just send help quickly. The back door is open. I need an ambulance. I live on St. Jacobs Lane."

"Can you tell me your name, please?"

"Please just hurry. It's hard to breathe."

The call clicked off.

Chapter One

Friday

From the apartment above *Signorino's Bakery and Brew*, James 'Mac' McLane stepped down the stairs and into the sweet atmosphere of pastry and coffee. Lizzy, the woman he considered to be the other half of his heart—perhaps even the better half—looked up from where she organized the dessert case. On the counter nearby were several fresh pies to be added for the next day. He took in her fluid movements and her perfect backside as he absently buckled his belt.

She glanced up, caught his gaze, and let out a soft sigh.

"What?" he had to ask as he stealthily moved closer.

"There's just something about a man in uniform. It makes me feel all tingly and safe at the same time. I always think the uniform really fits you, but then I remember you could get hurt wearing it."

"I could get hurt stepping out onto the street whether I'm wearing it or not, especially if Johnny Hodgins is driving by." He made his way around the counter to her. His heartbeat picked up pace a little with her closer. He'd been with her seven months, sharing meals, sharing a bed, sharing his life in a way he never imagined, and still a fire ignited in his soul when she was within touching distance.

"Yes, I know. Doo doo happens everywhere."

He laughed at her choice of words. "I like your choice of words when you tell it like it is. You should get that made into a bumper sticker. You could make a million dollars."

She melted into his embrace. He closed his eyes, relishing the way she fit against him. Perfectly. Just touching her made him feel complete.

"I don't need a million dollars. I already have everything I want right here. And, if you decide you've changed your mind and no longer really want to be Chief of Police, you can help me in the bakery. I won't make you wear a gun—or a uniform, but you can if you want. Maybe just an apron. And nothing else when there are no customers."

"I'll keep that in mind." He had no idea how many times she'd offered or how many times he'd replied just as he did now. She no doubt knew he couldn't give up being a cop. He didn't even know if it was possible. For now, he held her close, lost in the soft, flowery scent of her hair, and swore he felt her heart beating with his.

"Be careful out there." Her whispered words weren't quite absorbed into his shirt. It was more like they were melted into his chest.

"I will."

"There's a storm coming. By the looks of the radar weather, its a doozy." She nodded toward the television attached to the wall in the upper corner above the counter. The sound was muted but red still flashed across the screen with the weather report of a huge storm on the radar.

"I see that. You stay safe, too." He kissed the top of her head. "Spend the night in that little man cave I put in the basement. The couch is comfortable. Keep your cell charged and with you and get some rest while I take care of the night watch."

It was her turn to say, "I will."

He said nothing about the fact her promise was false. He knew every time he took the night shift, she slept with one eye open, if she slept at all. He also knew these words they seemed to repeat every time he went out to do a job where he might not come back to her were urgently needed by both of them. Just as his next ones were. "I love you."

"I love you back."

He kissed her. Then he leaned against her, resting his forehead against hers as they simply stood, eyes closed, listening to the sounds of one another's breaths, and feeling their hearts beating.

A strong gust of wind pushed its way in and blew the napkins on the counter when Mac opened the door to step out onto the front walk. As she stood in the doorway, he grasped her folding chalkboard sign that had informed John Q. Public of Mossy Point that today's coffee special was called Springtime in the Forest. He had no idea if it tasted like a forest or not. He preferred his coffee bold and black. Lizzy knew that and didn't care if he ever tried her specials as long as he was there in the morning to share a cup with her.

Mac handed her the sign and allowed her take it in so the storm didn't blow it away. Then, after another quick touch of lips, Lizzy closed the door and he stepped lightly to his truck. A low rumble of thunder slithered through the air like cold fingers before he started the engine. Mac watched her lock the door. He gave her a wave. She pressed her palm against the glass of the door. The next growl of thunder was closer.

Chapter Two

Distant thunder rumbled. Quinton Worthington paused in closing his fly to listen. If they left in the next fifteen minutes, he might be able to drop Shelby off at home and make it back to his rental before the storm dug its claws in. Across the darkened living room, Shelby Burns slipped her hot pink tank top over her head. He liked watching her dress.

He liked watching her undress more. Truth be told, she was a little dumb, but she had curves, she moved with the grace of a dancer, and she could be a regular sex machine when she was in the right mood, which was almost always. What was even better was she was almost always open to try new things.

Quinn had no trouble envisioning her spinning around a pole, swinging her blond hair, her great tits moving with her. She always wore hot little thong panties, too, just as he imagined pole dancers wore. One of these days, he was going to have to visit one of those clubs, just to compare and know for certain. Shelby caught him staring at her and smiled, slow, as hot as her panties. Then she ran her tongue over her bottom lip, reminding him just how she knew to use that tongue fifteen minutes ago. Then seeming to float across the room, she drew closer. Her kiss and her tongue tickling his sent fire all the way to the pit of his stomach.

If they hadn't already spent so much time in the house, he'd go another round. But their experience four nights previous left him leery of overstaying their welcome. Kind of. The truth was he had never felt so excited about living on the edge. He was a king, a god. He could do whatever he wanted, however he wanted and no one could stop him.

He wondered where in hell Trish and Josh were. They'd left the living room some time ago. He had hardly noticed when, because Shelby was doing such wonderful things with her mouth. In fact, it hadn't bothered him in the least, but now it did. They were in this together. They were a foursome. Usually, they had their fun together so if someone wanted a quick switch or to just watch the show instead of being a participant, he or she could.

Now that he thought about it, Trish and Josh, more and more, were playing singles, out of sight. He didn't feel so good about that. Because, even though he really enjoyed everything Shelby did with him and for him, Trish was sweet. And if he wanted a fast grab or a kiss or if he wanted two at once or he simply wanted to watch what she did with Josh, he couldn't very well do that if they were in another room. Shelby didn't seem to notice. Or care. She was like the curvy engine that could. And did. In fact, she did everything he asked, plus some. He really had no reason to complain. She kept him well satisfied.

Yet, Josh and Trish left him feeling miffed. They had no right to change the rules without asking him.

"Where are you going?" he asked when she ended her hot exploration of his mouth and headed toward the darkened stairs.

"Upstairs to see if I can find a fun trophy. Don't worry, I won't mess anything up." Her footsteps were loud, but then faded as she reached the upper floor.

Quinton watched until she was swallowed by the dark upper floor. As soon as she was out of sight, he pulled out a small bit from the tiny plastic bag in his pocket, and took a hit, letting it melt right on his tongue. He'd been told not to do it that way, but he'd discovered it was the best high after all. How dare that idiot lie to him. Besides it wasn't a big taste. Hell, he was still feeling the high from the one he took to get the party started. He closed his eyes, let his drug recipe slide through him and invigorate him.

After a deep breath, he stepped lightly into the kitchen where he found Trish and Josh at the table, fully dressed and looking well put together, as if they never took their clothes off, as if they hadn't just spent the last hour fucking each other's brains out. But then, since he hadn't watched them, perhaps they hadn't. He found that idea burning in him like a lit cigarette put out against him down in his gut. Between them, they shared a glass bottle of pop—cola. They didn't know he was there. He took the opportunity to watch them. Josh swallowed a big gulp before sliding the bottle across the table to Trish. Her drink was more delicate. They were so in tune with one another, they didn't know he watched them until he cleared his throat to get their attention. The sound was followed by a louder, closer, sound of thunder.

"What are you guys doing in here, having your own little private party?" He didn't even try to hide the sarcasm.

For a long moment, he didn't think either of them was going to answer. He added, "Hell, considering the way you have the table between you, it doesn't even look like you two have been kissing. And what's with the sharing the soda?"

"There were only two in the fridge. We thought someone might notice if they were both gone," Trish explained.

"That's doubtful, considering the old lady who lives here is probably not getting out of the hospital for a while. If at all. Considering the stroke we saw her have."

"This is why it felt a bit weird doing anything here." Josh finished off his explanation with a swallow from the bottle. "I told you I didn't want to come back here after the other night."

"Are you kidding?" Quinn chuckled as he asked. "This is the best place to be. No one is going to come here. No one is going to catch us. No one is going to care if we cook a buffet. After all, we were kind enough to call nine-one-one on her phone and save her life for her. She should thank us by allowing us to cook and eat whatever we want here. By the time anyone comes around, all they're going to do is clean out the fridge and toss it all in the trash."

"It still doesn't feel right." Trish gave him a hard look before taking a drink of the soda, leaving enough for Josh to finish.

Josh finished off the drink in one long guzzle and set the bottle on the table with a heavy thud. "And I think Trish and I are ready to go. You guys can stay as long as you want."

Shelby chose that moment to traipse into the kitchen. "Look at this pair of fabulous boots I found."

Everyone looked at Shelby's legs, her skinny jeans tucked expertly into a pair of what appeared to be genuine rawhide black, tall boots which just reached her knees. She carried her running shoes, which Quinn thought was rather ironic considering he doubted she'd ever run if some big monster chased her.

"Why do you always have to take something?" Trish asked.

Shelby shrugged nonchalantly. "What difference does it make? The lady who lived here clearly stroked out. When, and that's really if, she ever comes back here, I doubt she's going to be thinking about wearing these boots. I might as well enjoy them. Besides, it's spring. These are something you'd wear through most of the winter. She isn't going to miss them until next October."

"Actually," Trish corrected, "those are riding boots. She might be looking for them the next time she thinks about going riding a horse."

Shelby gave her a hard, frustrated, narrowed look. "Do you see a horse around here? Trust me, they were in the back of the closet in a second bedroom. She's not going to miss them. Why shouldn't I enjoy them? Especially when they fit me perfectly. Just like this."

Shelby held out her hand revealing a diamond and ruby ring on her third finger.

"Aw, shit. Do you really think something like that won't be missed?" Trish moved closer and studied the ring. "I'll bet it's some sort of family heirloom. Put it back where you got it."

"And I'll bet it's nothing more than fake stained glass. Why have you started to rain on my parade so much?" Shelby's voice softened, became sweetly seductive. "Is it because I haven't shown you a good time lately? Is it because I've given all my attention to Quinton? Are you missing my tongue action?"

"No," Trish replied without hesitation. "Josh is doing just fine on the tongue action."

Quinn took the opportunity to interrupt. "Speaking of which, I thought we were in this together. I thought we made a pact, a vow. We're all partners here, and yet, it seems like the two of you are going off on your own. I mean I haven't touched Trish or watched either of you in a few weeks. So, what's the deal?"

Josh and Trish looked at one another as if some sort of mental communication crossed between them. As if they made the psychological decision that Josh should speak for them, he said, "We've kind of become accustomed to just the two of us. And I've asked her to marry me."

A blaze of anger ripped through Quinton, like a forest fire in fall started with a can of gasoline, before he could stop it. A closer, but still distant, rumble of thunder seemed to accentuate it. "Need I remind you, this little foursome was your idea?"

"We know," Trish put in quickly. "And we enjoy it, we really do. And it was great when we were out under the stars up by Marston's Tunnel or in the woods on a blanket or up on our favorite ledge. But this breaking into people's homes...every time we do, I'm enjoying it less and less. I'm so afraid we're going to get caught. The thrill of the sex gets lost in the worry over it. And then when that old lady caught us the other night...and then fell over and hit the floor right over there. My God, I thought she was dead. I thought we killed her, even though we didn't touch her. I can't let that happen again."

"Yes, well, we had to think of something when it started getting cold, right?" Quinton thought he did a good job keeping the anger out of his words. "None of this seemed to bother you last November, remember?"

"Ah, that's sweet," Shelby finally chimed in. The smile on her face, however, was still directed at the obvious great find she had in the way of new boots. "You're a poet, and didn't even know it, Quinn."

Quinton ignored her. But she grabbed everyone's attention a breath later as she exclaimed, "Damn, there's paint on these boots.

Would you look at that? Someone put red paint on there. I didn't see that before." She put her foot on top of the table directly between Trish and Josh, and missed kicking over the empty bottle of soda by inches.

For a long moment, the room was quiet as everyone stared down at the deep red paint that graced the outside of the right boot on the back of the heel. The paint appeared to have been put there purposefully, for it was in the shape of a small X.

"I can't see why you're so worried. I thoroughly check every house before we enter. I always do my homework." Quinn bit back a surge of laughter that welled up in him at that statement. He hadn't done any fucking stupid homework since last December. He was done doing homework and planned to never have to do it again.

"Yeah? Did you thoroughly check it the other night when that woman came through the back door to find you fucking Shelby on her kitchen table?" Josh's voice held an I-told-you-so ring that rubbed his gut like sixty-grit sand paper.

"I'd watched her for weeks. She'd never left BINGO early before. Obviously, she didn't feel well and came home early. She was geared for a stroke anyway."

Then Josh stood. "We're leaving." His attention was directed at Trish. "Are you ready?"

"Yes." She stood, too.

"We're not through talking." Quinn was so proud of himself for keeping the anger that boiled through him unseen, he had to fight the urge to puff out his chest.

"We are for now. Besides, there's a storm coming and I want to get home before it hits."

Josh and Trish slithered out the back door before he could stop them. Their actions reminded him of a two-headed snake, two heads, but moving as one body.

"Let's go," he ordered Shelby.

"Did you straighten the living room?" she asked.

"I don't care. Let's go." He found it was true, he didn't really care, not just then. He cared that Josh and Trish walked out, that they were *getting married.* How dare they? Did they plan to continue including Shelby and him? No one left Quinton Worthington behind standing in the dust. Ever.

He thought what the four of them had was good, something that would continue for some time, like an unending party. Their little secret get-togethers left him exhilarated and feeling like a part of something very special. The last thing he wanted to see was part of it walk out the door. And while Shelby was a great lay, he liked a little variety. He didn't know if he could ever marry anyone, be devoted to one particular person; but if he was, it wouldn't be Shelby. She was used to fancy things he didn't plan to provide, as given by the boots and the ring and other trinkets she always swiped. She seemed to easily recognize expensive. And while he made cash—quite a bit actually—from the little sideline job he created in his basement in the way of his own tweaked drug recipe, he didn't plan to share it, at least not with Shelby.

Josh and Trish were already gone by the time he and Shelby closed the back door behind them. He watched the taillights disappear around the bend through the trees of the drive as he stepped off the porch.

Shelby looked up at the dark sky. "The rain's coming fast. We probably won't make it home." She high tailed around to the passenger side of his truck and jumped in.

He followed suit. Before he slammed the door, he turned to her. "So what?" Like he cared about the weather. What was a little rain? Thunder rippled around him as if to remind him it would be a little more than just rain. He didn't mind the thunder either. What he didn't like was change, or someone else calling the shots when it came to him. He didn't like that Josh had just driven off.

"So, I don't want to get these new boots wet. And I don't need my hair frizzing."

Leave it to Shelby to be more concerned with boots and hair when their party was obviously breaking up. He noticed she rubbed her hands over her breasts. "What's the matter?" he asked as he started the engine. "Your tits need more attention or did you put your bra on backwards?"

"I think you left those little ring things on too long. They kind of hurt."

"You liked it when I did it," he pointed out, not seeing any sense in apologizing for it.

He shot down the drive, spitting gravel into the air and moving fast enough to send the rear tires of his small pickup truck fishtailing as he maneuvered around the curve of the drive.

"Why the hell are you driving so fast?"

"I'm going to catch Josh. We need to finish our conversation." He envisioned a shark gnawing at his gut when he thought about the possibility of never getting to kiss Trish again or party with them. From the first time they'd ever done their little party sex thing, he'd known he could never do single sex again. There was simply nothing better than watching someone else while he was doing it, too.

Shelby said nothing as he sped down the highway. She still said nothing when the first huge raindrops plopped on the windshield or when the rain quickly turned into a torrential downpour. He turned on the wipers as fast as they could go, but it didn't help to see any distance. Not that it mattered, he recognized Josh's taillights. But when he drew close, she asked, "What are you going to do? Ask him for the key to his trunk?"

"Shut up."

"Can you even see? Because I can't. Now knock it off!" Before Shelby could see it coming, he swung his hand and back-handed her, striking her left cheek.

Burning pain had to be instant in her face because it left his hand feeling like it vibrated. He saw her eyes watered in the same instant. He doubted anyone had ever hit her before. And he knew the shock of it was probably enough to tilt her world. But she needed to be taught a lesson on who was in charge here. She brought her hands close to her face.

In the mere glance Quinn sent her way, the ruby ring sparkled on her finger as if it was filled with inner fire.

Her voice was beginning to grate on his nerves as much as the idea of Josh and Trish going their own way. "What the fuck? You prick."

"Shut up, or I'll give you another one. That's for trying to tell me what to do. You *never* tell me what to do. Understand? I see fine," he lied. "I know you like a little pain, so don't act like my hitting you was any big deal. And if you say another word, I'll open the door and shove your ass out."

There wasn't a car in sight in either direction. He pulled out into opposite lane and sped up enough to move alongside. Using the control on the door handle next to him, he rolled down Shelby's window.

She followed his instruction and said nothing, but she used her own button to put it up.

Quinn ignored Shelby and put it back down, and yelled out to Josh, who he could barely see through his own closed window and the dark. "Pull over!"

Josh's window went down. "Are you crazy? Not here. Not in the storm, not with the rain. We'll carry this on somewhere else."

Quinn laughed. "Like where? At your house with your dad in the kitchen? My dump? I don't think so." He wasn't about to let anyone in his house close to his lab.

"I don't know, but not here!"

Quinn slithered closer.

"What are you doing? Knock it off!" Josh yelled.

Shelby screamed as he eased his front bumper against Josh's. The rain had them moving slower than usual, otherwise it would have been more than just the minor scrape it was. "Are you fucking crazy?"

Josh screamed the same thing at him.

Quinton laughed.

Suddenly a car came out of the storm, headlights cutting through the sheets of rain, close.

"Look out!" Josh yelled.

Shelby screamed again.

In SMALL TOWN STORM, lightning will strike twice. While the storm of the decade beats down on the town of Mossy Point, Chief of Police 'Mac' McLane has his hands full. Two young people are missing. One of his trusted friends just lied to him. A young woman has mysteriously acquired new jewelry and can't seem to get her story straight regarding the bruises on her throat. How can Mac keep his town or the love of his life safe when streets are under water, trees are down, and the power's out? And it seems there is no end to the storm...

Find Small Town Storm on all platforms where books are sold.

About the Author

Allie Harrison lives in Southern Illinois. When she isn't creating the next great character and dropping him/her into another suspenseful situation, she's biking, camping, enjoying family time, or getting lost in the latest best seller. You can find her on facebook or at allieharrison.com